Seeing Dead Things

A Paranormal Women's Fiction Novel

Roxie's Midlife Adventures book 1

Leigh Raventhorne

D1412352

The characters and circumstances in this story are a product of the author's imagination, and represent no real person, living, dead, nor undead. Any real public places or names are used only to build an atmosphere for the reader's mind.

Chapter 1

I walked out through the sliding glass door that led from the family room to the back deck, and then down one step to the pool level. Okay, stomped out might have been more like it. I was furious. I wanted to cry, I was so hurt, and I needed some air.

How much longer are you going to put up with this crap Roxanne Bonacci-Bell?

We'd had yet another disagreement turned shouting match over Her Royal Highness Michelle, Steven's spoiled twenty-two-year-old daughter from a previous relationship. She'd recently graduated from Ferris State University—barely—with a degree in partying as far as I could tell, and had moved in with some guy with a philosophy major, who was having trouble finding work in his field in Michigan.

Imagine that!

Fast forward a few months, and they'd been evicted from his apartment, wherever that was, and had shown up here unannounced. Without even bothering to ask me what I thought about it, Steven had offered for them to stay here in *her room* for as long as they needed, to "get back on their feet."

Stunned, I threw the brakes on at that. "What? Hold the phone everybody," I announced. "Don't you think you and I need to talk about this Steven? In private?"

"No, I don't," he answered bluntly. "My daughter is welcome in *my* house *anytime*. I don't need your permission for that!"

Oh, I may just light him on fire for that! I thought. *He said that in front of them too. His house? I don't think so. And I don't even know Pencil Neck's name.*

"Oh, I am *so* not listening to this shit," Michelle spouted. "C'mon Brad, let's go upstairs and let Dad's wife throw her little fit."

There it was. Brad. "Get the hell out!" I shouted, moving between her and the staircase, pointing at the door. Brad's eyes got wide, and he immediately headed for it.

"Now see what you've done, you bitch?" Michelle screeched as she followed him.

She'd always sassed me, and Steven had always let her get away with it. I'd married him almost ten years ago. I was thirty-one then. He was thirty-nine. Michelle had lived with her mother and had visited us every other weekend while she was 'growing up'. The weekends from hell is how I eventually began to think of them, but I'd kept my mouth shut. For the most part. If I said anything, I'd get blasted with, "You're not my mother. You can't tell me what to do! Daddy!!" and the crap-show would start. It wasn't worth it, but I told myself it was only every other weekend and a few holidays. I could get through this for a few years. Things would get better, right? Not. Steven and I hadn't been happy for years. Most of that was centered around Her Highness, but it seemed that nothing I did pleased anymore, either.

We bought this place the year Michelle graduated from Grand Blanc High School. Go Bobcats. Steven thought that more room to spread out, and the beautiful pool out back would make life more fun for all of us. But Michelle had never lived here. She'd only visited. And when she did, all through college, she brought a gaggle of girlfriends and their almost non-existent, teeny bikinis with her to lounge around the pool all weekend. I evolved into the maid on those weekends, waiting on Princess Michelle, her entourage, and my husband—who needed his eyes glued back in his head. He seemed to enjoy the scenery just a little too much.

All that ran through my head and refreshed my memory as to *why* I didn't want her moving in here, especially now! I wouldn't be caught dead in anything other than a one-piece swimsuit these days. No way was I going to be made to feel self-conscious of my forty-year-old body in my own home.

Steven shot me a look and chased after them. I heard some words exchanged, a car engine started, and the car drove away. He came back inside and slammed the door, his angry eyes cutting straight to me.

That's when I decided to go out back for some air. I just needed space to breathe. Steven and I didn't normally argue much, but when we did, it almost always centered around Michelle. Of course, we also had the usual disagreements about money and all of the things that most couples experienced. We would get it out of our systems, cool down, and move on. In the early years, there was even great make-up sex after. These days, not so much. We had progressed to polite cohabitation—mostly.

However, the look on his face as he threw open the sliding glass door so hard the screen fell off its tracks, told me this wasn't going to be one of those times. In fact, it kind of scared me a little, but I'd be damned if I would let *him* know that. He practically ran over to where I stood, but I held my ground, arms crossed to show my disapproval.

"Who the hell do you think you are, running my daughter off like that?" he *screamed* in my face. I could feel his breath and tiny droplets of spittle hitting my skin, he was so close. "I am *sick* of your fat ass enjoying the free-ride around here and treating Michelle like shit whenever she's here. Those days are over! Do you hear me? Over!"

"How could I *not* hear you Steven?" I fired back, but reservedly. "I'll bet the neighbors over on the other side of the subdivision heard you just fine. Lower your voice, and you watch your mouth, mister!"

It was far from the first time he'd said mean things like that to me while angry, and the frequency had noticeably increased of late. But he'd never really frightened me before. Not like this time. I unconsciously found myself taking a half-step backwards, uncrossing my arms, and planting my hands on my hips instead for a little more balance. That decision prevented me from reacting in time to something he'd never done before.

Almost like it was happening in slow motion, his body leaned back a bit from me and turned slightly away from me to his right. My mind didn't process what was happening until it was too late. I saw his right fist approaching my face, then stars exploded in front of my eyes! I didn't really feel anything at first. I did notice that spit, and I guess some blood went flying out of my mouth as my head snapped backwards. Quite a bit of blood actually. I could feel myself falling backwards, my hands still at my sides. One of my hands came up belatedly to try to protect my face. There was no way I was going to be able to break my fall. I do remember that thought flashing through my mind.

Please don't let me fall in the pool and drown!

It was close. I hit head-first on the cement coping that edged the built-in pool. That made another round of stars explode in front of my eyes. My whole body bounced, but at least I didn't go into the water.

Thank God!

My vision blurred, but I could still see Steven. His face looked horrified at what he'd done. No . . . maybe not! Something big, dark, and very fast flew over the top of me with a tremendous snarl and flattened Steven where he stood. That's what had horrified him. He'd seen it coming.

Asshole! You deserved that! I hope it really hurt too!

Then the pain kicked in. I spit out blood and drool with my last conscious thought. Blurriness filled my entire range of vision, and blackness followed. Lights out!

I vaguely remember hearing a yell and loud noises. I remember being dragged away from the pool by the sleeve of my blouse, until it ripped.

I can't believe he hit me!

That was it. All I remember. Good night.

Chapter 2

I woke to a rhythmic beeping noise and a voice that sounded familiar talking quietly in the background. Everything hurt, and it was dark. My head felt like it was in a vise. Like literally in a vise—I couldn't move it! Panicking, I tried to open my mouth to call for help but the sound that came out was little more than a moan.

"Rox? Oh my god! Are you awake, Rox? Tess, I've gotta go, Roxie's waking up."

That voice. I knew that voice.

"Roxie, I'm here girl. You're in the hospital. Everything's okay. You're going to be okay. Just try to stay still."

That was Sam's voice. Thank god! Wait, what did she mean stay still? I couldn't move for Christ's sake! And why was it so dark? My face felt odd and—wrong, somehow. Why couldn't I make anything but these weird moaning noises? And why was that beeping noise getting faster.

"Hey Roxie, can you open your eyes, sweetie?" Sam asked softly. She sounded like she was right next to me. I could feel her brushing my hair back from my face.

Why can't I open my eyes? Why can't I talk?

I tried turning my head toward her voice, but I still couldn't move it. My neck hurt something awful. I heard a hissing noise and felt pressure on my leg. What the hell was going on? Scared and angry all at once, I did the only thing I was pretty sure I could still do. I started crying.

"Mrs. Bell? I need you to calm down," an unfamiliar voice said. "I know you are probably confused. You're in the hospital. My name is Connie and I'm the nurse assigned to you for this shift. You can't talk right now because you suffered a broken jaw. We had to do some minor surgery and wire it shut. You're going to be fine; you just need time to heal. I need you to calm down and breathe. Your blood pressure is a bit high right now, but we don't want to give you any meds for that if we don't have to."

I felt, well, I didn't know how I felt. Scared, for sure. But why couldn't I open my eyes? It felt like they were glued shut.

"I'm going to lay a warm washcloth across your eyes for a minute," Connie went on. "Your eyes are probably dry and might be difficult to open. This will help."

A few moments later I slowly opened my eyes. Everything was a little blurry. The nurse—Connie—was standing off to one side, checking over an I.V. bag filled with—something and hanging it up somewhere out of my range of sight. Sam's face suddenly appeared, blocking out everything.

"Way to scare a girl, Rox," she said. "Do you remember what happened?"

I felt, rather than saw, Nurse Connie shake her head in my periphery.

I made a noise that sounded more like a grunt than a moan. I must have injected just enough derision in it because Sam had the grace to look a bit sheepish.

"I'm sorry, Rox! Sheesh. We have to figure out a way for you to communicate. Connie, can we undo her hands for a little while?"

"Let me check with the Doctor and we'll see. We have to keep her hands away from her face and head right now, so she doesn't unintentionally do more damage or dislodge anything. It might not happen today, since visiting hours are almost over, but maybe tomorrow."

I must have blanched because Sam immediately tried to reassure me.

"You are going to be fine, Roxanne. You've got a concussion and we had a bit of a scare that there was minor brain damage from bleeding and some swelling. Your jaw is going to heal, but like the nurse said, it's going to take time."

Sam was going into full-on lawyer mode; I could already tell. I was still in shock that I was in a hospital.

What the hell happened to me? Had I been in a car accident?

"You've been in an induced coma for almost a week now, until they could get the swelling under control," she continued. "Between that asshole hitting you and the knock your head took on the side of the pool, you were in pretty rough shape. Do you remember any of that?"

"Ma'am, she may not remember much of what happened to her right away. That's very common for head injuries like this. And that's okay," Connie said as she moved into my line of vision.

"It will probably all come back to you, but we don't want to push you too hard in the beginning," she continued, slanting Sam a stern look. "These things take time; you can't force any of it."

"Roxie, that bastard will get what's coming to him. When I'm done with him, he won't have a pot left to piss in!" I had never heard my best friend sound so furious! She was renowned in the courtroom for being cool under fire.

"Ma'am, please!" my nurse warned.

I didn't know what to think at this point. My vision was clearing up some. Things weren't as blurry now—but I was confused. And I still hurt all over.

"I'm going to angle your bed up a little more, Mrs. Bell—"

"Not for much longer!" Sam interrupted.

The nurse just sighed and continued, "Ma'am, can you blink your eyes for me?"

I did as she asked.

"Good. Now, are you in any pain?" she asked. "Blink for me one time if you are, two times if you feel your pain level is tolerable."

Well, this felt cliché. I blinked once.

"That's normal for what you've experienced. I'm going to give you a pain reliever in your I.V. It will make you feel sleepy. And your friend here will need to leave shortly."

"Wait!" Sam looked at me, flustered. "I still need to talk to her!"

My eyebrows rose. At least, I think they did. My whole face hurt, so it was kind of hard to tell. Weren't pain meds supposed to kick in fast through an I.V.? No sooner had the thought crossed my mind than my eyelids suddenly felt heavy. I vaguely heard Sam talking to the nurse as I floated into darkness again.

***

I came to with an odd sense of Deja vu. The pain wasn't nearly as bad and I could open my eyes, at least. I could see Sam pacing at the very edge of my field of vision, her phone to her ear.

"I don't care what other cases have to be moved, Tess, just do it. Clear the rest of my docket and give all of the associated files over to Frank. He should be able to handle my clients for the next week or two just fine. Lord knows I've had to do the same for him more than once."

Sam, you've never missed a day of work. What are you doing?

I must have made some small noise because her attention snapped right to me.

"Tess, I've gotta go, Roxie's waking up again. If anything more comes up or if Frank gives you any crap, text me," Sam instructed her assistant. "I'll let her know. All right. Yes. Bye."

Sam slid a chair over closer to my bed, angled so that I could see her.

"Hey, Beautiful. How are you doing today? You look more alert," she said brightly. "You've been in and out of it for the last few days."

What? Days?

It felt like only hours ago. I remembered waking up and some, if not all, of what she and the nurse had told me.

"Unh!" *Shit. That seemed to be the extent of my current vocabulary.*

"Oh, and Tess says 'hey'," she went on. "She says to hurry up and get better. She has a new recipe for wine slush and can't wait for you to critique it."

"Unh?" *Ugh! This was already tedious!*

"Rox? The nurse should be back in here in just a few minutes . . . they don't want me to push this right now, but I've got to ask," she paused, chewing on her lip. "Do you remember any of what happened?"

"Unh, unh," *Was she kidding me right now? How the hell was I supposed to answer her? My freaking mouth was wired closed.*

I paused my thinking for a moment. What did I remember? Not much. The harder I tried to remember, the worse my head hurt. I started to shake my head, but it was still immobilized. So, I did the only other thing I could think of—I blinked twice.

"That's okay, it will come back. In the meantime, we just have to work on getting you out of here."

At that moment, another nurse came in. She looked over a whiteboard on the wall, checked the monitors, recorded something in the computer, and then finally looked over at us.

"Well, it looks like our patient is finally awake again! And her vitals are so much better than they were a few days ago," the young woman said. "The doctor also said we can undo your arm restraints. Just try not to touch your head or your face."

After she undid the straps, I slowly reached over and massaged my wrists. I hadn't even realized they bothered me. Of course, I immediately wanted to touch my face to figure out what was going on there. I huffed out a sigh and would have rolled my eyes if I hadn't thought it would probably hurt.

"When will the doctor be back in to see her?" Sam queried.

"I believe he should be making his rounds within the hour."

Paying only partial attention to Sam talking to the nurse, I turned my mind back to Sam's earlier question of me. I closed my eyes for a moment and tried again to remember what happened. There was an angry face for just a moment, something dark and fast, then . . . nothing.

Steven! Where was he anyway?

Maybe he was at work. He was a skilled tradesman at one of the local General Motors plants. It seems like he could have gotten the time off to be here, though. Maybe he'd already been and gone? As these thoughts flitted through my mind, I felt a strange flash of fear, and my stomach clenched.

The nurse did a few final checks on the numerous wires and tubes coming from, well, every part of my person it seemed, and then left.

"As soon as the doctor gets his *very* fine butt in here and talks to us, we can figure out a decent way to communicate. I brought you a tablet and an e-pen, so maybe that will work better for us now that you've got your hands back. One of the evening shift nurses said it can take some practice to learn to speak with the jaw hardware. And they have internet here! It's slow internet, but hey, it might help stave off boredom."

I made a weird snorting attempt at a laugh and nearly choked. My bestie didn't always sound like the top-notch lawyer she was. She looked tired, though. I wondered how long she'd been here by my side. It sounded like I had been here for—what, a week and a half maybe? I held my hand out and mimed writing.

She rifled through the attaché next to her and pulled out a tablet, charger, and one of the pen thingies—an e-pen?—for it. *Ugh.* Sure, I was almost 41 years old, but I didn't consider myself technologically challenged. I had a degree in journalism from MSU and had worked in the court system in one capacity or another for well over a decade until Steven had pushed for me to stay home. Seriously though, what was wrong with good old pen and paper?

Sam continued, "There are some books loaded on here, too, plus my Kindle Unlimited account. You can read when you feel up to it. Download anything you want. Oh, and there are cards and flowers here from Annie, Tess, and all the girls from the office. Cammie even made you a card."

My eyes teared up a bit at that. Annie had been Sam's housekeeper for nearly as long as I had known Sam. She was also a great friend to us both, as was Tess. Cammie was Annie's special needs daughter who had stolen all of our hearts from the day she was born. She had a heart just as big as her mother's.

"The girls stopped up to see you, but you were still out of it. They'll probably wait until you're out and have had a chance to recover a bit before they converge on you."

Sam was almost babbling—and she was *not* a babbler. She had also been sneaking furtive glances at the door the whole time she was talking. What was up with that?

Chapter 3

Sam looked over at the door as someone else walked in. Luckily, I was at an angle that I could kind of see the door. This no-turning-my-head thing was already annoying after only twenty minutes of being awake.

"Great! You're awake! How's our patient today?" the young man—who looked as though he might have been in his very early thirties—asked with a beaming smile. Yes, beaming. I had always thought of that term as an exaggeration until now. If I could have turned my head away from that one thousand-kilowatt smile, I would have.

Without waiting for an answer, he pulled a pen light out of his pocket and proceeded to blind me as he thumbed my eyelids up and shined it into them several times.

"Good pupil response," he murmured. "How's the pain level today?"

Automatically, I start to answer. To my absolute horror, I felt drool running down my chin.

Without missing a beat, he gently wiped it away with a tissue he produced from somewhere outside my periphery.

"Don't worry, that's perfectly normal," He said with a wink. I'm pretty sure I went beet red. "Having your jaw wired is no picnic. Believe me, I know. I had it done myself as a teen. I'm Dr. Lane, by the way. Leo Lane. I specialize in head injuries. Your Maxillofacial Surgeon was in earlier, probably while you were still out of it. She'll be back to check on you again tomorrow but, according to her notes, it looks like your jaw is doing great. No permanent cosmetic damage. You're lucky. You might only be wired up for about four weeks instead of the usual six. Once you are able to eat solid foods again, you'll just have to take it easy for a few weeks."

Four weeks of not being able to talk and drooling like a teething baby? That was lucky? How was I supposed to eat? Wait! Did he say when *I'm able to eat solid foods again?*

Dr. Lane must have noticed my distress. It might have been the tears and hyperventilating. "Hey, it's okay," he reassured me, patting my hand. "You are going to be perfectly fine. This will be one of those things you look back on and laugh about some day."

Sam grabbed my other hand and gently mopped at my eyes with another tissue. My always-first-to-take-charge friend had gone strangely silent since the doctor came in. That thought distracted me from thinking about my own problems. I side-eyed her, since that was pretty much all I could do. She was blushing. Huh, go figure.

Looking back at the doctor, I studied him a bit more closely as he continued talking. Thick, dark hair. Eyes just a shade darker than what I would call stormy gray. He was wearing scrubs and a lab coat, but I could still tell he took pretty good care of himself. His chiseled face had the faint beginning of a five o'clock shadow, giving him a slightly rugged look. It was hard to determine from a hospital bed but I thought he was decently tall. Yeah, he was definitely a hottie.

"Your last MRI looks good. All of the swelling around the brain as well as the fluid buildup is gone—you must be quite the fast healer. It doesn't appear that there will be any permanent damage. You may experience headaches and a few other residual side effects. I'll have a nurse go over all of that with you before you're released, though. I'm going to have a nutritionist come in and talk to you about your new diet later today, too. We may be able to pull your feeding tube by tomorrow."

Feeding tube? My hands immediately flew to my mouth, my inspection of Dr. Hottie forgotten.

Dr. Hottie, er, Lane gently pulled my hands away. "The tube is actually in your nasal passage. Sounds gross, I know, but that's how it's done."

Ewww! Now that he mentioned it, I could feel some pressure from the tube. My whole nasal passage felt odd and, swallowing, I felt what must be the tubing. I immediately wanted it out.

"Once that tube is out, you will be able to talk. It will definitely take some practice talking around the hardware," he made a small gesture to indicate my wired jaw, "but you'll get there faster than you know."

Sam piped up at that moment. "Does the four weeks include nine days she's been here?"

"Great question," Dr. Lane said, turning his attention to my friend. "Unfortunately, Dr. Rhea - the surgeon who operated on

Mrs. Bell's jaw—will have to answer that, though. She'll have the final say depending on how quickly Mrs. Bell continues to heal."

I watched the interaction between the doctor and Sam, not really paying as much attention to what was said as they continued to converse about my recovery. At forty-two, she was no slouch in the looks department. She was often mistaken for at least ten years younger, unlike me. Nobody ever mistook me as being less than my forty-year-old self. She was slightly taller than my own five foot-five inches, and about thirty pounds thinner than me. She ran several miles every morning—outside, if the weather was good, or on a treadmill in her workout room if it wasn't. She tucked her long, blonde hair behind one ear, and I saw Dr. Hottie's eyes follow the movement. He crossed his arms and relaxed into his stance. I noticed he didn't have a ring on his left hand.

Sam likes Dr. Hottie . . . and he is definitely responding. Interesting.

I forced myself to tune back into their conversation. "So, barring any objections from Dr. Rhea, or any further issues, we may be able to release you within a week." Dr. Hottie—I mean Dr. Lane—was saying. "I see Ms. Stone—"

"Please. I told you to call me Sam," she interrupted, practically purring. I did a mental eye roll.

"Sam, then," Dr. Lane smiled at her. "I see she brought you a tablet. Great thinking." He was addressing me, but his eyes didn't leave hers. "If you want to write down any questions you think of or let us know if you are in any discomfort, that would be helpful."

He finally turned his full attention back to me. "I'm going to have the nurse come back in and remove some of the bracing around your head and neck so that you can move a bit. Just take it easy. Your neck may be sore for a couple more days but that's perfectly normal for what you've been through. I'll check on you again tomorrow, Mrs. Bell." He patted my arm lightly, nodded at Sam, and exited the room. I saw Sam's eyes follow him all the way out.

I grabbed the tablet and the pen-thingy and started writing. First things first . . .

-WTF happened to me Sam???-

"Oh, Rox, I was hoping you would remember," Sam said after reading my question. "I don't know all the details. Just that Steven . . ." she paused. "As your attorney, I can't take the chance of influencing your memories of anything that happened." She must have seen the confusion in my expression because she stopped my hand when I started writing down my next question, giving it a gentle squeeze before letting go again.

"What I can tell you is that you were found, unconscious and bleeding, next to your pool. You were rushed here and have been in an induced coma long enough for the swelling on your brain to go down. There was some bleeding in your brain, but that seemed to have resolved itself while you were in the coma," she paused, swallowing hard. "Roxie, you scared the crap out of me! They were talking about drilling into your skull to relieve some of the swelling and the pressure from the bleeding."

Sam took a deep breath before going on. "They had to bring someone in to wire your jaw back together. It's broken but it isn't as bad as it could've been. You've got plates and screws in there, holding everything together until it's healed. You've been here for nine days now."

I thought about what she was telling me. And I thought even harder about what she *wasn't* telling me. I needed to remember what happened, that much was plain. There was that flash of fear again. I shivered a little, which felt really weird when you couldn't move your head, by the way. Huffing out a little sigh, I started writing again.

-Where is Steven? Why isn't he here?-

She looked away, not meeting my eyes. "We'll talk about that when you can remember more."

Well, that was vague. What is it that she can't tell me?

I erased the previous questions to make room for the next.

-So what's up with Dr. Hottie?-

Sputtering, she answered, "I don't know what you're talking about."

-I call Bullshit! -

"Leo, er, Dr. Lane is just . . ." She sighed and lowered her voice to a whisper. "Okay, fine. He's hot. But he's at least a decade younger than I am."

-And???-

"And what? I'm too old and too busy right now."

-As if that's ever stopped you before. He couldn't take his eyes off you. Just saying. -

She palmed her forehead, shaking her head. "Roxie, seriously. This isn't about me, here. We need to focus on you. My dating life, or lack thereof, can wait. Let's just work on finding out what happened that day and getting you out of here."

-When was the last time you slept? -

"I've napped in the chair over in the corner. It reclines."

Knowing her, she hadn't left my side except for bathroom breaks and quick trips home to shower. I remembered her conversation with Tess as I was waking up.

-Go home and rest. Please. I'm fine. -

She didn't say anything for a minute. Then, "Are you sure?"

-YES! And do something with your hair before Dr. Hottie sees you again. -

Laughing, she smacked my arm lightly. "I love you, girl. I'll be back first thing. If you remember anything, anything at all, about what happened, write it down and save it in a file on the tablet."

-Will do. Love you too. Go."-

After Sam left, I realized I was exhausted. She had plugged the tablet in to keep it charged—luckily, it had a really long cord—and tucked it in the bed within easy reach. Closing my eyes, I listened to all of the sounds in the hallway. How did people get any rest in a hospital, anyway?

That was the last thought that I remembered before I was out again.

Chapter 4

Terror. Pain. A snarl, and something huge charging at us—

I woke with a start, breathing hard. It was kind of dark and I didn't recognize where I was. Confused, I immediately tried to sit up, only to find that I couldn't move my upper body. My hands flew out, only to hit metal bars. I heard the clatter of something falling onto a hard surface. And beeping. What was that infernal beeping?

"Hey, hey. Mrs. Bell, you're in the hospital. It's okay. You're okay," a woman in scrubs hurried into the room. She grabbed one of my hands and began gently rubbing it. "I'm Connie, do you remember me?"

I blinked once. It came back to me in a rush. I had a head injury and a broken jaw. I managed a groan as I recalled everything Sam and the doctor had told me.

"I know. It can be confusing for the first few nights waking up in an unfamiliar place." Her eyes were so kind, I immediately relaxed.

My other hand dropped onto something in the hospital bed next to me. The tablet. I fumbled around, feeling for the pen. Connie, stooped down and picked it up off the floor, placing it in my hand.

"Is this what you're looking for?"

One blink.

I turned the tablet on and started writing.

-Sorry. Nightmare.-

"Ah. That's okay. You've been through a lot, so that's normal."

-Sam?-

"Your friend? She's barely left your side since you've been here." *I knew it!* "She just left again, maybe an hour ago. We've been letting her stay past normal visiting hours, but I told her to go and get a real night's sleep. That chair is *not* comfortable enough to actually sleep in."

-Good. Thank you. Do you have a mirror?-

"Oh! Umm . . . I - I don't," she stammered out. "I'm sorry."

-Is it that bad?-

"No! No, of course not. I mean, there's some bruising. And your head is still bandaged. You were so lucky they didn't have to shave your hair. You've got great hair!"

It must be pretty bad. She's babbling now and she won't look me in the eye . . . I decided to let her off the hook.

-Are you here to take my head and neck bracing off?-

Relief flooded her face. "Yes, I can do that. I saw the orders for that earlier."

She proceeded to unlatch a brace from around my neck. What a relief it was to have that thing gone. Next went the brace around my head. I slowly moved my head side-to-side. It was sore, but tolerable. I don't know if it was my imagination, but I could feel the feeding tube against the inside of my throat even more now. Just the thought of it made me gag.

"Go easy. You'll feel some stiffness and you might be a bit sore."

A bit? Understatement.

-When will feeding tube be out?-

She gave me a sympathetic look. "Probably not for another day or two. You'll have to, um, learn how to eat again. And it's going to be smoothies for a little while until you work up to soft foods."

One final question . . .

-Has my husband been by?-

"No, ma'am. Not during any of my shifts, anyway," she said quietly. "Do you want me to check with any of the other shift nurses?"

-No. Thank you.-

***

The next few days dragged by. The nutritionist came in and talked to me about how the next two weeks of my life would look like food-wise. Connie wasn't lying about the smoothies! Dr. Rhea visited twice to check over her handiwork and to give me tips on talking and managing the drooling. Basically, I would need to have a small towel handy at all times. Dr. Hottie, er, Lane, stopped in daily to check my head—and to flirt with Sam, who was there more than she wasn't. My feeding tube was finally removed, which was a truly gag worthy experience. I was pulled out for a couple more scans. I read a few books. Nobody would give me a mirror. I even tried to see my reflection in the tablet screen, but it had a matte finish protector. Too bad it wasn't the kind with a camera built in. Sam refused to bring me my cell phone.

By this time, I had been in the hospital for just over two weeks. I was having nightmares nearly every single night. It was always the same thing each night—a general feeling of fear and pain, then something big and dark sailing over me. The funny thing was, the big dark thing wasn't what scared me . . .

Sam kept me entertained daily with her stories about the daily drama at the office. How did I get so lucky to have a friend like her?

Tired of reading, I set the tablet down and thought back to how we had met. I had finished my degree in Journalism and Communications at MSU and come back home, overly optimistic about finding a job in my field right away. Turned out, it was so much harder than I thought it would be! I put resumes out all over the place. With the exception of an offer to become what amounted to a glorified coffee girl at one of the local papers, there was nothing. Becoming somewhat desperate as time went on, I finally began looking for anything that would give me a paycheck. I replied to an ad for an assistant in the legal field. No experience required, will train, it said. Sam interviewed me the next day, hired me on the spot, and we became fast friends. From the first day, she never treated me like I was just an employee—it probably helped that we were so close in age. She was fresh out of Law School and had just passed her Bar Exam. We worked out of a tiny hole of an office in downtown Flint. I found that I loved working in the legal field. We both put in long hours and watched the practice grow quickly. Before long, she brought in a partner, relocated to a large, newly renovated building, and had an office full of paralegals and assistants.

We spent most of our weekends together during those early years. We went wine tasting at some of the vineyards popping up all over northern Michigan, went on beach vacations, cruises, kayaking adventures . . . We were practically inseparable for the first few years. She had even been there when I met Steven at the bar near the office, where several of the legal staff had lunch together almost every week.

My stomach immediately knotted at that memory and I heard the heart monitor on the side of my bed speed up. I tried to draw a few deep breaths—which was not easy to do with your mouth wired shut. I had to draw in through my nose and whistle it out through my teeth. The monitor slowed to it's normal rate.

What was up with that? I dismissed it as anxiety, trying not to think too hard about why. I already knew from experience that doing so would lead to a blazing headache later.

***

"Guess what?" Connie asked brightly, walking into my room and shutting the door behind her.

"You got me. What's today's torture?" I enunciated as carefully as possible, mopping gently at my mouth to contain the mess. Talking was getting easier but it sounded like I was speaking through clenched teeth. Probably because I was.

"Your catheter comes out and you get a real shower!" She smiled like I had just won the freaking lottery.

"Uh, what?" I knew I had a catheter. A nurse, sometimes even a male nurse, came in to empty the bag and record the output. I knew they dealt with this stuff every day, but, *ewww*. Things *were* getting irritated down there and I desperately wanted it gone but...

"You heard me." She had washed her hands and was gloving up now. "It's time. You've been on your liquid smoothies for a couple of days now. You graduate to a slightly thicker diet today, so you have to be able to use the bathroom. And won't a shower feel good? No more of that dry shampoo Sam's been using in your hair?"

What fresh hell was this? Like I hadn't been completely humiliated with the daily sponge baths already? I nearly had a heart attack during the first one. A male nurse had presumably drawn the short straw. Lucky for both of us, Sam had been present and knew me well enough to send the young man out and request female nurses only for this task in the future. After he was sent away, relief clearly written all over his face, she had laughed hard enough to nearly wet her pants. She actually had to go check.

This was my first experience with a catheter, so I had no idea how it worked. Then a thought occurred to me. Who had put it in? I had been unconscious. I broke out in a sweat and could feel my face flush.

"Roxie," I had asked her to call me that instead of Mrs. Bell. "It will be over before you know. There is nothing to be embarrassed about. I do this all day. Along with bedpan duty and much, much worse. You will feel so much better with that thing out of you. Believe me."

I went to that place that I'm sure all women my age escape to during procedures like this and tried to tune what was happening down there completely out. What were the first ten numbers of Pi? Three point one four one five . . . something.

"Take a deep breath and let it out slowly, Roxie," Connie instructed. I felt a tug and a pop. "There! All done. See, that wasn't so bad. The trick is—" she held up a small bottle proudly in one hand and the cup-like contraption that must be the catheter in the other.

How had that even fit up there?

"Proper lubrication and easing it out slowly. Makes all the difference in the world."

If she said so . . . although it did feel better. The discomfort I hadn't even acknowledged with everything else going on was now mostly gone, but I wasn't sure if my happy place would be happy again any time soon.

Connie disconnected what must have been about two dozen cables hooking me up to the various monitors. Then she unhooked me from the I.V. stand, capped off the I.V. leading into my arm, and helped me sit up. A wave of dizziness had my head spinning.

"We're just going to get you used to sitting up for a few moments. When you're ready, we'll walk over to the bathroom."

I waited for the room to stop tilting as she moved my legs to the side of the bed. From there she helped me stand and we hobbled over to the bathroom. Finally, a mirror! I was shocked by my appearance. My eyes looked bruised and there was bruising around my mouth and jaw. My lips were chapped and peeling. My normally thick, dark auburn hair, despite Sam's best attempts with dry shampoo, looked lank and greasy. I squinted at the thin streak of steel gray that stood out right at the front. That was new. *What the heck?*

Connie hustled me over to the shower. "Do you think you can stand okay on your own?"

"You going to shower with me, Connie?" I snorted.

She laughed. "It wouldn't be the first time I've held a patient upright in the shower." She proceeded to point out the bars to help me support myself and how to work the shower itself. There was even a little seat in there. "I'll help you undress and then I'm going to take the monitor tabs off before you get in. Your skin is going to be irritated but the shower will help. When you're done, we'll moisturize you, get you into a fresh gown, then it's back to bed."

After I showered and washed my hair, I couldn't believe how much better I felt. I would never take showering for granted again. Connie began working lotion into my parched skin while I got a really good look at my upper body in the mirror. Had I lost weight?

I mentioned this to Connie, trying to ignore the fact that I was naked as a . . . whatever you call a naked thing. My mind went kind of blank.

"You went almost a week with nothing but nutrients through an I.V., and almost another week with a feeding tube. You've probably lost about fifteen pounds or so. That's common. Don't worry, as soon as your jaw is back to normal, you'll likely gain it back."

Worry? I was ecstatic. I had been trying to lose the stubborn twenty pounds that had creeped on since I got married for years now. Ten of that was gained after Steven made me quit my job. That and the stress eating whenever I had to deal with my stepdaughter.

Thinking of Michelle made me uneasy, for some reason, but it didn't surprise me in the least that she hadn't been up to visit me. I pushed my thoughts of her away, tuning back into what Connie was saying.

"I'm going to put new patches for the monitors on again, placed next to where the old ones were, then we'll get a fresh gown on you."

I was holding the minuscule white towel I had used to dry myself with in front of me while she did all of that. Connie did her best to respect my modesty, but this was more than a little different than the monthly spa visits Sam and I used to treat ourselves to. Speaking of spa visits, I saw the condition of my legs. They were in desperate need of a razor. As were other areas.

Once I was back in bed, exhaustion hit me hard. I was out before Connie even finished hooking me back up to everything.

And I woke up screaming.

***

"Write down everything you remember." Sam handed me the tablet and pen. "Even if you don't think it important."

"I know the drill. Probably better than you. Don't you have a pen and some real paper in there?" I asked, pointing at her attaché. I was angry and trying hard not to take it out on her. I knew why she hadn't been able to tell me what happened before I could remember it on my own. The clues had all been there, I just had to let my psyche catch up. Plus, there were the legalities.

Sam handed me a notebook and pen, saying nothing. I immediately felt ashamed for snapping at her.

I closed my eyes and breathed slowly out of my nose. Mainly because if I did this with my mouth right now, it resulted in a whistling noise. I could not *wait* to have this hardware removed in two weeks.

"He's seriously in jail? What happens now, Sam?"

"Yes. Now, you focus on you. Let me take care of everything else. I just need your statement. You might have to answer some questions from the police, too. The rest will take some time, but you know that." She paused, then asked more gently, "You're sure about this, right?"

What other option do I have? I nodded, feeling sick. Steven's fist coming at me and the sound of my head hitting the edge of the pool kept going through my mind, over and over. I couldn't go back to him.

"You are going to be fine, Rox. Better than fine. You are so strong. And I will be with you every step of the way. He won't know what hit *him* when I'm through with him." Her vehemence didn't surprise me. She and Steven had never truly gotten along. He had seemed great about our friendship up until we were married, then anything that took my attention away from him became an issue.

I sighed. There were lots of other forty-year-old divorcées out there, many far worse off than me. I could do this. Right?

When Sam had showed up this morning, I asked her about the new addition to my hair. She'd shrugged and said that it must be from the head injury. Trauma perhaps.

"If it bothers you it can always be covered up. When you're up to it you can schedule an appointment to have your hair done or maybe we can do a spa day. Personally, I think it gives you a rather edgy look."

Edgy? That was a word I would never have used to describe anything about myself. I decided not to worry about it for now. I had too many other things on my plate.

Chapter 5

The next week flew by. I gave my statements, both to the police and to Sam. I decided to leave out the part about the—whatever it was—that I was now convinced had scared Steven away. It was the one thing I really had no idea how to explain. I didn't allow myself to consider how much worse it would have been had he not been scared off.

Dr. Rhea was pleased with how my jaw was healing and would remove the latex and outer hardware holding my jaw together in another week. It freaked me out that the screws and metal plating used to repair the jaw itself were permanent. She assured me that I would still be able to go through metal detectors without issues and that I wouldn't even know that they were in there. Other than that, I just needed to be even more meticulous than I already was about dental hygiene from now on. Oh, plus no hot liquids and no alcohol for at least another week. I honestly don't know which bothered me worse. I was dying for a cup of coffee, even a cold one.

The day finally came for my release from the hospital and Sam was right there for me, just like she had been the entire time. I didn't know how in the world I could ever thank her enough for everything she'd done for me through all of this. When they wheeled me to the front door in a wheelchair, her red Cadillac was already waiting to pick me up.

"Get in. Time to bust you out of here girlfriend!" she teased.

"I've never been so ready to leave a place in all my life," I groaned. "The question is—what am I supposed to do now? I don't think I'm ready to go back there. What happens when Steven gets out of jail? We both know they can't hold him for much longer. I can't believe he's been held this long."

"Oh, Sweetie . . . no worries. He will probably get out on bail soon, but there'll be a personal protection order in place before he does that keeps him well away from you, or he goes right back to jail. He's the one who won't be able to so much as come to the house to get his stuff," Sam assured me.

She chewed her lip for a moment, then continued, "By the way, you've given me temporary power of attorney until you were out of the hospital. It was a bit of a liberty, I know. I also notified your bank of the situation and was able to put a temporary freeze on the joint accounts. It won't hold much longer but it was the only way to slow Steven's chances of making bail before you got out. I was able to convince the judge he was a danger to you and high flight risk, so bail was set really high. His, um, *daughter* has been raising quite the fuss about it, though. In court and out."

Processing this took a moment. "Thank you Sam. I think I will take you up on your offer to stay with you for a while, after all. I need real sleep for a day or two before I even have to worry about going to the house and . . . everything else. In the hospital, every time I shut my eyes, somebody came in to poke me, prod me, or to check if I was asleep! And those machines, with the constant beeping! How a person is expected to get any actual rest in a place like that, is beyond me."

We both mulled over all that she had told me as we drove the short distance back to the entrance of my subdivision. We did a drive-by past my house. Everything looked perfectly normal from the outside, so we headed to Sam's house. I've always felt very comfortable there. Even though her place is directly behind mine, it's practically from an entirely different era. It was the original farmhouse on the land that part of, if not all of, my subdivision was built on. Having always been single, with plenty of cash to blow, she'd made a real showcase of it. She had told me once before that it was built in the nineteen-twenties and, as was the custom back then, it was a big two-story box with lots of bedrooms upstairs. At some point between when she bought it and when my house was built, she'd had the entire upstairs remodeled into two luxurious bedroom-suites on either side of the central staircase. Each suite contained its own large bathroom with heated tile flooring, gorgeous garden tub, separate shower, *huge* walk-in closet, and a reading area.

Sam's room was done in deep pinks and the other—the one I would be staying in—was all soft yellows and glossy whites. Obviously no compromising with a man over colors here.

I'd always said that the only taste Steven had was in his mouth. He always insisted that every wall be painted eggshell or beige. "Neutral colors are better for resale value." *If he'd said it once, he'd said it a hundred times. Boring!*

Up in my room, I sat down in the extra-deep, overstuffed, soft Italian leather loveseat in front of a large window overlooking a wooded area. For being near such a large subdivision, I couldn't see any other houses from this window.

I can decorate like this now, too, I thought. *After what he did, we're through. I'll never forgive him for that.* Unconsciously, my hand went to my mouth, which was still slightly swollen. *Oh, who are you kidding Roxanne? You're forty—almost forty-one. You have no job to speak of anymore. And you're going to be divorced. How will you even be able to buy the paint, let alone afford to keep the house? You'll have to let Steven have it, or sell it, or—something.*

With those revelations, the floodgates opened, and there was no stopping the tears. I put my hands to my face and let myself cry it out. *Your marriage is over. You wasted the best years of your life on him.*

I had reduced my hours at Sam's law firm to the point I was only on-call or doing occasional contract work from home when they had heavier than normal workloads. *What was I going to do now?* I had loved my job at the firm, but being gone for so many years would mean that the office dynamics had changed. I wouldn't be in the same position I was before. Would everyone see me as a victim? That thought bothered me more than any other, I think. That brought on even more tears.

Sam came in and, seeing me crying, sat down next to me and hugged me tight. "Don't worry Roxie, it'll all work out. You'll see. Don't worry about it today. I brought you some pajamas. There are fresh towels in the bathroom and clean sheets on the bed. There's even a new toothbrush on the counter. How about you take a nice hot bath and get some sleep. Whenever you get hungry, just come downstairs. I'll whip us up some kind of creamy homemade soup for later and keep it warm. Just rest, Sweetie.

Yes. That's what I'll do. I'm lucky to have a friend like Sam.

***

The first day I was home alone at Sam's house, sometime after she'd gone to work but before the crack of noon, I came downstairs in search of food. Barefoot, I was still in the two-piece pair of pajamas I had left here from one of our girls' nights in. A quick glance out the window told me it was a gloriously bright, cheerful day outside. Assuming there was such a thing anymore. I walked into the kitchen heading straight for the coffee pot—Dr. Rhea had just said no hot coffee, but I knew where the ice cubes were—only to stop dead in my tracks. There was an old man sitting at the snack bar on a stool, looking out the window at my old backyard, smiling. I did my best attempt at screaming, but it came out more like a wounded pterodactyl's mating call, I think.

"Who the hell are you?" I demanded, working hard to enunciate through my jaw hardware. And to not drool.

The old man turned my way, seemingly unfazed by my behavior. "Hello there! My name is Elmer. Elmer Jenkins. I live here, Roxanne."

Okay, how does this old guy know my name? And why has Sam not mentioned that someone else lives here now? Where's my phone? Do I need to call the police?

I stepped backwards a couple of steps closer to the front door, in case I needed to make a dash for it. "Sam never told me about you. How long have you lived here?"

Elmer smiled at me calmly. He did have a kind and gentle look about him. "Oh, I've been here for over thirty years now, I guess," he said.

"That's not possible. What the heck are you trying to pull here? Sam's lived here for eight years now." *We didn't drink so much on our monthly wine tasting, movie marathon, and occasionally man-bashing weekends that I would have failed to notice an old guy hanging around, right?* And I distinctly remembered her telling me that her grandparents were dead.

"That's correct. I remember when she moved in here quite clearly. It upset me greatly, at first. I also remember when you and Steven Bell built that house over there, what was it—four years ago?" he asked, pointing vaguely toward my house. "Samantha bought this house from my children after I passed away, from my estate sale, you see."

Wait. What?

"Come again? Your what?" I asked.

"You know what an estate sale is Roxanne. After I died, my children sold my house and divided up or sold all of my belongings."

"Huh. You don't look very dead to me . . . Elmer. Am I losing my mind here? Am I really out of the hospital, or is this just some weird-ass dream?" I wondered, those last questions more for myself than him.

I moved forward quickly and poked him in the arm with my right forefinger. Not. My whole hand went right through his shoulder without touching a thing! My hand went ice cold. Cue up yet another, but somewhat better, scream.

"Roxanne, please!" he exclaimed. "Must you screech right in my ear?"

"Well . . . yes! Yes, I must! What the heck are you?" I asked, poking my finger into him several more times to various depths, ignoring the icy sensation this produced. "This can't be right!"

Elmer smiled his calm, amused smile again at me. "I'm a ghost, Roxanne. Or a spirit, if you prefer. I chose to remain here after I died. I had something important to do that kept me here."

Now I know I've lost my mind. A ghost. Riiight. This old man sitting here in Sam's kitchen expects me to believe he's—dead— and he's haunting her house? Nurse? Can I have more of those drugs? Wait. Did Leo, er Dr. Lane, mention anything about brain damage?

"And exactly what . . . important thing did you have to do that kept you here . . . Elmer?"

"Come in and sit down. It's kind of a long story."

"That's okay. I'm good over here. Wait. First tell me why Sam has never mentioned a little thing like the fact that she has a *ghost* living with her?"

He shrugged his shoulder. "She doesn't know."

I cocked my head a little at that, processing it. "And—why is that?"

"She can't see me."

"And yet I *can*. Tell me Elmer, *why is that*?"

"Must be that nasty bump to the head you took," he said with another shrug, "either when Steven punched you or when your head hit the cement and bounced a couple of times. I saw the whole thing, you know. Not that I can be a witness for you in court. Nobody else would be able to see or hear me."

"Wait. You saw it? All of it?"

"Indeed."

"So then maybe you can tell me something that I haven't been able to figure out, and apparently Sam missed."

"Try me."

"Right after Steven hit me and I fell down, my vision was all blurry. But I remember him looking at me—or something behind me—like he was completely terrified. I thought I heard something really loud, and I'm sure I saw something really big fly over me and knock Steven down. What was that?"

"Jake!"

"Jake?"

"Yes. Jake is my Newfoundland dog. I'm old and not very fast—even ghosts have limits—so when I saw Steven become violent with you, I sent Jake over to intervene. It appeared to me that Steven could hear Jake barking and growling as he came, but couldn't see him. I would imagine that *would* terrify Steven. Jake is—I mean was—a big fella! He used to go one-hundred-fifty pounds at least."

"Used to. Was. Is Jake a ghost too then? A ghost *dog*?"

"That, he is. Jake? Come here boy. Let Miss Roxanne see you."

Right next to me a huge black dog with long black fur poking out all over appeared. The thing was the size of a pony! Or maybe a bear. He nudged me gently with his snout. Not. His snout passed right through me. I felt a definite and instant chill, but nothing physically touched me. I'm kind of ashamed to admit that I may have wet myself a tiny bit.

Oh, the joys of being forty . . .

I pulled out a stool on the opposite side of the snack bar and sat down on it with a thump. "Please explain to me why he can't touch me, yet he was able to knock Steven flat on his a—, erm, butt?"

"Oh, sure. Spirits *can* make physical contact with the living, if they really want to, but it takes a *lot* of their energy. It's much easier to just make the living hear us, but Jake knew he had to stop Steven from hurting you even more, so he just did what he had to. He needed to rest for several days afterward in order to regain his strength. He's no young fella himself, you know."

I turned and looked at Jake. I started to reach out to pet his massive head, remembered I couldn't, and pulled my hand back. "Thank you Jake, for doing that for me," I told him. I started to relax, just a little. Then it hit me— "Shit. I'm seeing dead things."

***

We spent most of the day talking, until I realized what time it was. Sam would be home from work soon and here I was, still in my pajamas. I excused myself and went upstairs to shower and get dressed. My life kept getting weirder and weirder by the day. Freaking unbelievable!

When I came back downstairs, Elmer and Jake were nowhere to be seen. And I did look for them. And call them. Nothing.

Do I dare mention this to Sam, or will she have me put away somewhere for being batshit crazy? Yeah . . . No! Better that I keep my mouth shut. For now. Ghosts. Who would have ever thought? Am I nuts?

I got a text from Sam that she was five minutes out, with dinner. We were experimenting with different foods put through the blender. And being my crazy, ride-or-die friend, she was eating the same things I was, minus anything extra to soup it down, since she could actually chew. We had both crossed salad off the list of foods we could stomach eating this way. Though most of the chunky soups weren't too bad, watered down with broth. Tonight, it would be Whoppers from Burger King. And fries. Shaking my head, I settled into a comfy love seat in her living room, opened a magazine she had there, and made like I'd been lounging there all day.

***

The next few days followed nearly the same pattern. Elmer, sometimes with Jake, sometimes not, would sit and talk to me while I made my breakfast smoothie. He would occasionally answer the myriad of questions I threw at him.

Where do you go when you aren't here? What do you do all day? Are those the clothes you died in? You don't peek at Sam in the shower, do you? You don't peek at me in the shower, do you?

Those last two questions had him spluttering and blushing. He insisted quite vehemently he would never do that.

I spent the rest of those days on Sam's treadmill, watching television, reading, and looking up new smoothie recipes. Sam had brought my purse, laptop, phone, and a few essentials from my house. She had even changed the security code, in case Michelle tried to get in. I wasn't ready to go back there yet, but I knew I would have to suck it up and go sooner rather than later. According to Sam, the accounts were now unfrozen. Steven had managed to hire some hotshot lawyer and would be out on bail any day now.

Speaking of which, I had received a few interesting texts from Michelle. Some were from when I was still in the hospital, all were pretty much the same. Demands that I drop the charges against her dad and that I respond to her texts. Then a boatload of profanity and even a couple threats. There were several phone calls from her number where she hung up without leaving any messages. I ignored all of it, per Sam's advice. She told me not to erase the texts or the records of the phone calls. She would use them to prove harassment, if needed.

When the day finally came, Sam took me to Dr. Rhea's office to have my jaw unwired. I was almost disappointed in the process. With just a few snips of the wires, she undid the latex bands, looked over her handiwork, gave me a pamphlet with instructions, warnings, etc., and pronounced me good to go—call her if I had any issues. Her office would bill my insurance and send me a statement for what I would owe.

Chapter 6

"Roxanne—there are lots of other things out there besides ghosts like me. Dangerous things. Things you don't want to notice you."

"Like what?" I wanted to know more about my new world. Elmer had agreed to tell me what he could, so here we were, in Sam's kitchen. I fixed myself a breakfast smoothie. I was down almost twenty pounds now; no way was I going to put it back on without a fight—rinsed out the blender and sat down at the snack bar. He was sitting at the magazine-worthy farm table, Jake leaning against his leg.

"I don't know all of them. Heck, I probably don't even know most of them. I try to stay close to home for a reason. There's things out there that—," he paused, face scrunched in thought, "well, from what I was told when I was little and my Grandmam figured out that I was like her, with the Sight and all—there's things that can use someone with the Sight. Use them for bad stuff."

I had a million more questions, but I let him talk. I had my notebook out and figured I would write down anything relevant.

"See, the Sight was strong in my family. That's how it works. Bloodlines either have it or they don't. Some of them are strong with it while others can barely See," Elmer chewed on his lip for a moment. "The ones that are strong, they grow up with it and have to learn to hide it. Those that aren't very strong with it, they might only have it when they're little. Then they outgrow it and eventually forget about it. The things that those ones See are generally explained away as being part of an overactive imagination or whatnot.

"I think that was you," he went on, pointing at me. "I think you must have had at least a little of the Sight when you were a kid. And that knock to your head just flipped it back on, like a light switch. But I think it's stronger in you now than it's supposed to be. I can . . . see it in you. And if I can, then Others will, too."

Jake groaned and flopped over onto Elmer's feet. He bent down and rubbed the monstrous mutt's ears. That dog really did look like a bear. And he drooled more than I had with my jaw hardware. I looked down, expecting to see puddles on the floor under him, but it was completely dry. Weird.

"Did your wife know you could, um, See?" I asked, curious. I ignored that last thing he said, processing it.

"Oh, yes. She had a touch of it, too, I always thought," he said wistfully. "I sure miss that woman. Especially her voice. She could sing like a bluebird. She hated her name, so the family always called her Birdie."

"Did you two ever talk about being able to See things?"

"Sometimes. What I could See, she could only sense, I think. And once in a while there were things that she sensed that I couldn't See," he shook his head. "My Grandmam, she said it all came down to the blood."

"What about your kids, Elmer? Couldn't they See you after you passed?"

Shaking his head sadly, "No. It can skip a generation, sometimes two. I'm glad, though. They aren't in danger, at least. But I worry about their kids and their future grandkids. There won't be anyone to teach them any of this."

I thought about that for a moment as Elmer seemed to lose himself to his own thoughts. If the Seeing was passed down through families . . . Where had mine come from?

My parents had been older when they had me. They were both gone now, as were both sets of my grandparents. I had an aunt on my mother's side that lived down in NOLA, last I had heard, but she and my mother had never gotten along so I didn't really know her. She had sent several generous gifts for my wedding but hadn't attended. That was pretty much the last time I'd heard from her. I didn't know if she had any children or not, even. My mother had rarely mentioned her. I wrote a quick reminder in my notebook to touch base with her at some point. Maybe she would know something about all of this . . .

"So what else do you want to know Roxanne?" Elmer asked, apparently having snapped back to the present.

"Hmm. What other 'things' are there out there besides ghosts? That you know of, anyway."

"Well, there's the witches," he started, then chuckled at the expression on my face. My eyebrows had to be lost in my hairline. "You asked, girl. Now listen up. Witches. And not those kinds they call Wiccans that sit around knitting and singing Kumbaya out in the woods, pretending to pray to the moon or whatever. I'm talking about real witches. The kind that can curse

49

you, capture you, and suck your power down like a hot cup of tea. Or they will use you to find ghosts like me. Like most other things, there's good ones and bad ones. Mostly there's bad ones, though."

"Wait, wait—what do you mean suck my power down? And why would they want a ghost?"

"I don't know how they do it and I most certainly don't know why. I'm just telling you what Grandmam told me. If they catch you, they will use your power one way or another," he shook his head. "She thought maybe they could absorb or steal your Sight for a time and use it so they could see Others, too. But for some reason, they can't use it for very long. I saw a witch catch a ghost once. It wasn't pretty. She stuck him in some kind of a bottle thing, like he was a Genie. That ghost had been around for close to twenty years, always watching over his kids. I never saw him again."

Shivering, I wrote down everything he'd told me.

"Umm, okay. What else?"

"Let's see now . . . there's the Shifters, the Necroes, the Vampires, the Fae . . ."

"Vampires? Like *Dracula* Vampires?" I'm pretty sure my voice had squeaked up several octaves. Even Jake cocked his head at me. "And what is a Necro?"

He chuckled. "Yes, there are Vampires. There aren't a lot and I have never seen any around here, but they do exist. I've only ever seen one, in fact. Birdie and I went down south for a vacation one year, back in the eighties. She sensed him before I Saw him. I don't know how to even describe how I knew what he was . . . I just knew. I think that goes back to why the witches hunt us.

Anyway, that vampire, he knew us, too. He didn't seem to be interested in me much, but he sure homed in on my Birdie. Scared her pretty bad, he did."

"What, um, what did he do?" I asked, swallowing hard. This was worse than a ghost story.

"He didn't really do anything that I could see. But Birdie, she said he kept calling her, in her head, like. That he knew her name. Now, she said she didn't know what he was, not like I did, just that he felt . . . *wrong* to her. We didn't stay in town like we had originally planned. In fact, we drove two states over before she settled down enough to do more than keep looking out the back window."

This was unreal. Witches. Vampires. *Fae.* If it weren't for the fact that I was here, sucking down a smoothie, talking to a freaking *ghost* and his ghost dog - that had pretty much saved my life—I would have thought this was a weird dream. Or maybe a nightmare, as I considered the state the rest of my life was in.

"Having a hard time taking all this in?" Elmer asked.

"Yeah. Yeah, I am. It's a bit . . . much. I mean, you and Jake? I think I've had enough time to process you guys. And, I *thought* the rest would be less—" I found I was at a loss. "Just, less, I suppose."

"I think it's harder for the ones like you. The ones that didn't grow up Seeing the Others in the world. I was luckier than most in that I had my Grandmam and a couple others in my family to tell me what was what. And like I already mentioned, I had to learn early on how to hide what I could See from anyone who couldn't—especially back then. You can probably imagine what happened to people who could See things that regular people couldn't, right?"

I nodded, swallowing hard. "Were they hauled off to the loony bins?"

"Sanitariums. They did awful things to them in those places, Roxie. Electric shock therapy. Hydrotherapy. Heavy sedation and Psychotropic drugs. Isolation. And what's worse is that they became easy pickings for the Others."

"H-How do you mean?" I was pretty sure that I would never sleep again, at this point.

"Witches and some of the Others can hide in plain sight. They might look like you or Sam, or even your neighbors, but most of them are predators, don't you doubt it for a minute. They learned early on that sanitariums, hospitals, homeless shelters, places like those all make great hunting grounds. They could waltz right in, take what they wanted, and no one would be the wiser. A coven could even put one of their own in there as a doctor. It would practically be a smorgasbord for them." Now he was getting worked up, agitation marring his normally calm demeanor.

"A coven? Like, a group of witches? Elmer, now you *are* freaking me out!" My thoughts jumped to Steven. He did this to me! I didn't ask for this, to have to worry about being hunted by groups of witches!

"I'm sorry, Roxie. I know this is probably not how you pictured your life, even in your wildest dreams."

"Dreams? Try nightmares! What am I going to do? How am I supposed to even go outside? If they look just like everyone else, how will I know before they get me?" I was panicking, I knew that. I just couldn't help it.

"Roxanne, witches look like regular folk *to* regular folk. You will recognize one when you See her. And there are ways to hide yourself from some of the Others. Not all of them, though. We may have to cover that another day, if that's alright with you. I'm getting kind of tired."

Tired? How could a ghost be tired? I looked over at him, pushing my own anxiety over everything I had just learned out of my mind for the moment. He *did* look a little less glowy than normal.

"Are you okay, Elmer? Is there, um, something I can do?" *Smooth Roxie. Why don't you just offer to get him a glass of water? I'm sure that would be super helpful.*

"No, I just need to rest a bit. Recharge, I guess you could say. I'm not used to spending so much time on this side. We'll continue tomorrow." And just like that, he was gone.

All I could think to myself was that my life couldn't possibly get more weird. Note to self—do not challenge Fate. It will bite you in the butt.

Chapter 7

The next day . . .

I'd barely slept the previous night. Everything Elmer had revealed during our talk seemed to alternately terrify me and excite me. I wanted to know more—no, from what he'd told me, I *needed* to know more. My survival depended on it. I didn't doubt anything he'd said. He, or Jake rather, had saved my life. I trusted them both.

Dragging myself into the en suite bathroom, I took a quick shower and pulled my thick auburn hair back into an informal ponytail. I paused in front of the mirror, studying my reflection. Though I had dark circles from lack of sleep, all of my bruising had faded. Losing almost twenty pounds, coupled with no makeup and my pony, had changed my appearance more drastically than I would have thought. Despite my new gray streak and the other, less obvious gray slowly creeping in at my temples, I looked . . . years younger. Or maybe just less worn. What were they saying these days? Forty is the new thirty? I'd take it.

Dressing quickly in another pair of sweats borrowed from Sam, I grabbed my notebook and headed downstairs for breakfast. Rummaging through the fridge, I saw a new bag of spinach, a fresh container of strawberries, and Greek yogurt. It looked like Annie, Sam's housekeeper, and good friend to us both, had gone shopping. I hadn't even heard her this morning. I tossed what I needed in the blender, adding a banana and one of the nutrient packets Dr. Rhea had recommended I use—to make sure I was getting a 'complete diet'—from the bowl on the counter, and looked around for Elmer.

"Elmer?" I called softly, feeling foolish. "You here?"

Nothing.

At a bit of a loss, I finished making my smoothie, quickly cleaned up my mess, and walked to the sliding glass door at the back of the eat-in kitchen. The back of Sam's house faced the back of mine. Smiling ruefully, I thought back to how we had celebrated when I surprised her with the news that Steven and I managed to snag the lot for a great price. The building process was harrowing, requiring constant decisions—which, of course, spurred numerous arguments with Steven over everything from the layout of the kitchen to the brand of paint used on the walls. Sam helped keep me sane through it all.

Shaking my head, I knew I would have to go back to the house soon, for clothes and my own makeup, if nothing else. I sipped my breakfast, turning back toward the kitchen—only to come face-to-face with Elmer. I yelped and sucked a chunk of my smoothie down my windpipe.

"What. Were. You. Thinking?" I choked out when I was finally able to speak again.

"Sorry Roxanne. I didn't mean to scare you, but you seemed pretty lost in your thoughts there. I just figured I would let you find your way back in your own time," he *did* look truly remorseful.

"Give me a minute to let my heart slow back down."

"Take your time," he grinned sheepishly. "I thought I would show you something you might find interesting," he paused. "Something that might help you and . . ."

"And?"

"Well, I've been thinking about what we talked about yesterday. And about my grandkids."

His grandkids? What did they have to do with this?

"Um, okay," I felt more than a little lost here.

"You asked if any of my kids had the Sight. None of them did, but—I think one of them was like Birdie."

"Like Birdie?" Maybe it was still too early for me to have an intelligent conversation. My mind was scrambling to remember as many details as possible about his wife. Then it hit me. "Oh! Like with the Vampire? Like the stuff she could sense that you couldn't? Like that?"

He nodded. "Her name is Eleanor. We called her Ellie for short. She was our youngest child and was just like her mother in almost every way. She would be almost sixty by now."

Sixty. I remembered when that sounded so old. Crap, I remembered when forty sounded ancient!

"What makes you think she was like Birdie? What exactly could she do?"

"Just how she looked at the world. She noticed things that others didn't. She noticed some things before her mother did, even. We were never sure, mind you—we only suspected. This area doesn't have much in the way of Others. That's pretty much why my family settled here."

"Really?" That made me perk right up. "What about the witch that got the ghost? The one you told me about yesterday?"

"Oh, that was maybe fifty years ago, or so. I haven't seen a witch around here in a long time. Not that I get out much to look these days, mind you. But you still need to be aware of what's around you."

Relief flooded me. Maybe I would be able to sleep soundly again, after all. "I can do that. Now what were you going to show me?"

"Come on. We have to go upstairs. I'll meet you up there." He winked out, reappearing at the top of the staircase.

I huffed and puffed up the stairs, following him down the wide hall. I *really* needed more time on the treadmill. At the end was a door that I was pretty sure closed off the stairs leading up to the attic. I had never been up there—heck, I don't know if Sam had ever been up there.

"Are you going to open it? It's not as though I can," Elmer said with amusement.

"Oh! Yes, I can do that." I only hesitated a moment before turning the knob. I expected the door to creak open loudly, but it opened smoothly and silently. The stairs were narrow, inclining sharply. I could see light at the top, filtering in through one of the transom windows that were spaced evenly under the front and back of the roofline of the house. Funny, I had never really thought about those windows before, though I had noticed them. I guess I figured they were decorative.

I also noticed all the cobwebs and frowned. They looked fairly abandoned but one could never be too sure. *Freaking freeloaders.*

"What was that, Roxanne?" Elmer asked.

Oops! Did I say that out loud? "Nothing," I mumbled. "It's just that I don't really like spiders. When was the last time anyone came up here? Doesn't Annie, er, Sam's housekeeper, do any of . . . this?" I fluttered my hands at the staircase.

"The last time I recollect was when the contractors were here working on the remodel. Before that, it was probably when my kids moved some stuff up here before the house was sold. They came through and freshened the paint and redid the floors. I've never seen Annie come up here."

"Why would they move anything to the attic if they were going to sell the house?"

"I don't think they had planned to sell it outside the family originally. One of the grands was going to move in at one point but then had some financial problems and decided he couldn't afford the place. So, it was put up on the market. Birdie and I had really hoped it would stay in the family; you know?" His expression was so sad, I automatically reached over to hug him. Of course, when my hand passed through his shoulder, I withdrew my frozen fingers fast.

"Sorry 'bout that," he chuckled. "I know it's not pleasant. Done it once or a dozen times myself, back when."

"It's all right. My fault. So, maybe I should grab a broom or something? You know, for the . . . ," I waved at the webbing.

"You're okay with seeing ghosts, but you're afraid of spiders?" He seemed baffled.

"I'm not afraid! I just . . . don't like them," I insisted. Steeling myself, I started up the stairs, one hand in front of me to keep stray webs away from my face. The other hand kept a death grip on the rail while I carefully watched my feet all the way up. At the top I looked up and let out a squeaky scream when Elmer appeared in front of me.

"Elmer, if you keep that up, I'm going to be joining you in the ghost world when I have a heart attack! Or break my neck falling down these stairs!"

He shook his head at me but seemed distracted as he looked around.

Blowing my hair out of my face and brushing more cobwebs away, I turned and followed his gaze. There were quite a few boxes and totes up here, all neatly stacked against the far wall. I made my way into the room, ducking away from the sloped ceiling. The space looked as though it was divided into two areas. There was a door at the far end but, judging by the size of this main space, it must lead to a much smaller room.

Elmer started toward the door. Following close behind, I looked over at the boxes as we passed them. All were neatly labeled.

"Hey Elmer? Are all of these boxes from before? They don't look like anything of Sam's. And there are an awful lot of them."

"Yes, Roxanne. This is all mine from before I passed. I don't know how my children managed to forget about it up here. I guess they didn't want to be bothered with any of it."

Feeling awful for him, I wasn't quite sure what to say to that. I gave him a moment before I gingerly skirted around him to the door. "I take it that whatever you want to show me is in there?"

He took one last look at the boxes as he stopped behind me, careful not to make physical contact. Bracing myself, I turned the handle and pushed the door open. The room was much darker than the main area. I fumbled for a switch on the wall, finding nothing but a few cobwebs. I quickly withdrew my hand, wiping it on my pants.

"It's one of those pull cord types. It's in the middle of the room."

I reached forward, cringing inside as I felt around for a hanging cord. Finding it, I pulled. Breathing a sigh of relief at the instant illumination—I really hadn't expected the light to work after this long—I stepped further into the room. It was considerably smaller than either of the bedrooms on the second level and contained only two plastic totes and a large wooden trunk. I looked back at Elmer.

"Well?"

"The trunk. It's not locked. What you need should be toward the bottom."

Flipping the latch on the trunk, I lifted it carefully. Though the trunk looked old, it had obviously been well cared for. There was a gorgeous quilt on top, hiding everything underneath from view. I ran my fingers over it, marveling at the beautiful colors.

The patches of fabric were soft with tiny precise stitching. I gently lifted it out, surprised at the hefty weight, and laid it on top of the totes stacked to the side.

"Birdie's mother made that quilt for our wedding. Her family didn't have much money, so she never had a hope chest. I bought this trunk for her a few years after we were married, and we used it for memories."

"That's so sweet. And the quilt is simply . . . amazing."

I glanced back at him when he didn't respond. He just nodded at the trunk, but I thought his eyes looked a bit teary. Turning back to the task at hand, I began removing more, setting it all on the floor next to me. Several thick envelopes, a few framed pictures, a *huge* bible, four smaller blankets that looked handmade . . .

"Those were our children's baby blankets. Birdie knitted each one. Not a one of them wanted to take theirs with them when they left home."

I paused at one of the pictures. A much younger Elmer, dressed in a suit, stood tall and proud beside a petite woman in a formal white dress.

"Our wedding picture," he explained.

"She's beautiful. And you were quite the looker yourself!"

He guffawed at that, looking over my shoulder at the photo. "Oh, just look at my Birdie! She was the prettiest girl I ever met. When she smiled at me, I would darn near forget my own name."

I set the picture aside on top of the quilt. Peering down into the trunk now that several of the more bulky items were gone, I went back to work. A small wooden box came out next. The lid was decorated with beautiful designs and scrollwork. He said nothing about it so I kept going. In the very bottom was a small stack of books. They looked like—diaries, maybe? Or perhaps journals of some sort. They also looked old.

"Those are for you, Roxanne. For now, anyway. They belonged to my Grandmam. Some she wrote, some were written before her. Those were written by the women in my family."

"Y-You want *me* to have these?"

"Yes. I think you'll need them. They'll be able to tell you more about, well, everything, I guess. They're not doing anybody any good just sitting up here forgotten.

"I never read all of them, myself. Just bits and pieces. I wanted the kids to read them, so they would know what all was out there, but they were never interested. Even if they couldn't See what I could, I figured that if they at least *knew* about it, maybe they could teach their kids or grandkids. Just in case any of them got the Sight, you know? I would like for you to do me a favor though, if you would."

"Of course! Anything." *What was I thinking?* I wasn't. I had no idea if I would be able to do what he was going to ask or what it would entail.

"When you're done reading these, would you make sure my youngest gets them? My Ellie? And I think I would like Samantha to have the quilt. She's been good to this house, and to you. I think she would like it."

"Um, yeah. Sure, I can do that. And Sam will go nuts for this quilt! But, what about the rest of your things? Don't you want your kids to have any of this? Especially the pictures?"

He lifted a shoulder, shaking his head sadly, "They knew that trunk was important. And they knew what was in it. Ask them if you'd like, I'll leave that up to you and Samantha."

"All right. But, I do have a question. How am I supposed to track down Eleanor or any of the rest of your kids?"

"Didn't you used to work for Samantha's law office?"

"Technically, I still do, kind of."

"And didn't you ever have to locate people?"

I smacked my forehead with my palm, feeling stupid. *Maybe I can blame lack of sleep, head trauma, and the fact that I've been thrown into the deep end of the pool with no life preserver.* At the pool analogy, my stomach flipped in warning. Nope, I definitely wasn't ready to go there yet.

"How about I just give you their names and enough information to make it easy for you."

I narrowed my eyes at him. Now he was making fun of me. But I wouldn't turn down what he was offering.

I gathered up the books from the bottom of the trunk and then began carefully placing everything else back into it. As I picked up the beautiful little wooden box, Elmer spoke up again.

"You keep that. Its contents will no doubt come in handy for you at some point," he said, almost hesitantly.

"Oh. Can I open it up now?"

At his nod, I lifted the lid. There were several pendants and rings, a bracelet that appeared to be made out of leather and possibly hair, and a dried white flower. Picking up the flower carefully, afraid it would disintegrate, I studied it. It might have been a tiny rosebud, but I wasn't positive. I placed it gently back in the box and turned over one of the pendants. Startled, I almost dropped the entire box when I saw the opalescent stone front. It looked a lot like something my grandmother used to wear. I looked back up at Elmer.

"What is all this?"

"It belonged to my Grandmam. My cousin Rosemary gave it to me just before she passed and went into the light."

"I think I've seen a pendant kind of like this before. In fact, I'm pretty sure I have one just like it at my house."

"Have you ever worn it?" he asked, watching me curiously.

"No. It's just in with a bunch of other things that came from my parent's estate when they passed away. I don't remember ever seeing my mother wear it, though. Why?"

He was silent, still staring at me. I fidgeted nervously.

"There aren't many families that have these," he said finally.

"What do you mean?"

"Let's not worry about it for now, Roxie. How 'bout we call it a day."

I nodded, worried anyway, of course.

Making sure the trunk was shut tight again, I turned out the light and headed out into the main attic area. I stopped at one of the stacks of totes.

"What about whatever's in these?"

Elmer walked over and peered at the front of one.

"The label says glassware."

I rolled my eyes. "Thank you, Captain Obvious! I just meant, is there anything you want done with these or anyone you want them to go to?"

He shrugged, "Do whatever you want, or whatever Sam sees fit, with all of it. It belongs to her now. Some of those probably have the sets of Depression Glass Birdie collected. I think they might even be worth a little money these days. My children didn't want any of it or they would have taken it."

"Elmer, maybe there was a reason they didn't take any of it. Sometimes things happen or life just gets ahead of us. I'll talk to Sam about this stuff. I'm sure she would at least want to offer it to your kids. By your reasoning, this stuff," I held up the armful of journals and the wooden box, "belongs to her, as well."

He nodded, "Yes, you're right. But none of that stuff is going to do her a bit of good. You? It could very well save your life. I'll leave it up to you what you want to do with it." And with that he was gone.

Sighing, I took one last look around and headed back down the stairs. Well, I thought to myself, at least I was getting some cardio in.

Chapter 8

The next day flew by quickly. I only saw Elmer and Jake once, sitting on the steps to the back deck. Elmer seemed lost in thought and, when I tried to talk to him, he suggested I read through the journals, reserving any questions I had until after I was done. That was kind of out-of-character for him, but I thought perhaps the trip to the attic had upset him, so I gave him the space he seemed to need.

The journals were disappointing to say the least. They were barely readable, a jumbled mishmash of notes with no apparent order. It was almost as if different people had randomly chosen places to scribble down their thoughts, stopping and starting again, without the proper use of punctuation. Many of the notes were little more than accountings of what had happened to whom, not really detailing much. It was quite confusing. A handful of the entries even appeared to be in some other language.

The smallest of the journals consisted only of hand-made drawings of what appeared to be the contents of the wooden box, one per page, with odd notes penciled in all around them, but the majority of the pages were blank. The etched details on the wooden box matched the ones drawn on the cover of the journal.

Between the drawings and the matched details, I figured the two must belong together as a set.

The most detailed drawing was of a pendant from Elmer's little wooden box. It stood out from the rest as I flipped through the pages. I tried to make out the writing scattered randomly around it but, though the characters appeared neatly written, they were either so tiny I would need a magnifying glass to read them or this wasn't a familiar language. Maybe it was time to reconsider the reading glasses I had been putting off for over a year now?

The wooden box lay tucked in the nightstand drawer. I took it out several times, opening it and looking at the jewelry more closely as I paged through the matching journal. There was a very unique leather bracelet which had etchings of a variety of different animals burned into it, all around the band. There was hair woven around the band in a tight braid. It seemed to consist of a mix of different colors and textures, so I would guess that there was more than just one type of hair used. I flipped back through the journal with the drawings looking for it, but I didn't see anything like it in there.

Putting the bracelet back, I moved on to the pendant that looked a lot like my mother's—well, mine now, I guess. Examining the solid back, I could feel something stamped into the gold, but it was very faint. I noticed the edges of the frame holding the stone were etched, too. I flipped it over. The stone cabochon on the front was beautiful. I didn't know if it was a real opal or not— if it was, I had never seen one this large. Turning it this way and that made the fiery colors inside the stone dance. I ran my thumb across the front. Maybe it was my imagination, but it felt warm.

There were two more pendants, each with a different type of stone, just as impressive as the first one. I didn't have enough knowledge about jewelry or stones to even guess at what they might be. Both also had stamps on the backs and etched frames. One was gold like the first pendant, the other was a tarnished silver. The gold looked real, so the silver probably was, too.

Moving on to the rings, I plucked out the largest one in the lot. The stone was a soft pink in a chunky silver setting. Like the other pieces, it was engraved around the band. Curious, I slipped it on the ring finger of my right hand. Surprisingly, it fit. Deciding to leave it on for now, I sifted through the remaining rings. Two had delicate gold bands very similar to each other, just with different stone settings. They looked like they matched two of the pendants. There was also a tiny, delicate ring done in gold and silver woven together in an intricate pattern to form the band. The weave continued, circling around the top to form a small dome where a stone would normally sit. The overall effect was unbelievably elegant. It was more art than jewelry. By contrast the last ring in the box was a simple, crudely made circle of silver.

Returning the box along with the matching little journal to the drawer, I grabbed *my* notebook and started trying to make sense of the other journals again. Maybe if I took notes I could make better sense of them. I browsed through one that looked newer than the rest, looking for a date or a name of whomever had written it. I couldn't find either. I moved on to the next one. Again, nothing. That seemed odd to me. If these were journals or diaries, there should be something about whomever was writing it, shouldn't there? There were a lot of other names mentioned, along with who—or what—they had Seen or encountered.

Frustrated, I set the journal down. What was it that Elmer thought I would learn from these? They were just—a mess! And the timelines were so different, how could they possibly help?

Stifling a yawn, I realized I was exhausted. The rest of the journals went into a sturdy book bag I'd found tucked away in the closet, and I slid them under the bed. I had time to lay down for about an hour or so before Sam would get home. Tonight was just going to be a salad night, so dinner prep wasn't really an issue. With that thought, I was out.

***

I sighed and rolled over, not wanting to get up yet.

"Takes a lot out of you, doesn't it?"

My eyes flew open at the unfamiliar voice. "Wha- How did you get in here? Who are you?" I scrambled out of the bed.

"You called me here. The name's Rosemary."

Gaping at the portly woman, dressed in a seriously outdated outfit, standing in my bedroom, studying me—I was at a loss for how to respond.

Did she say I called her?

"You just going to sit there with your mouth hanging open, letting flies in?"

Snapping my mouth shut, I slowly stood. "Um, hello? I-I'm Roxanne."

Rosemary snorted, "I don't care who you are. I just need to know why you called me here."

"I'm sorry. I'm confused," I looked around for my phone. Had I somehow called some stranger while I slept? Was that even possible? I had heard of people doing weird things while they were on sleep medication, but I didn't take anything like that. I hadn't taken so much as a painkiller since leaving the hospital.

"That makes two of us, then, doesn't it? If you don't need me for anything, send me back."

"B-back?"

"Speaking isn't one of your strong points, I take it?"

Now wait just a minute. Who is this person to show up and just start insulting me? Chin high, I drew myself up to my full five foot five and one-half inches. "Speaking actually *is* one of my strong points. Give a girl a minute to wake up, will you? Now, would you please explain yourself?"

Rosemary gave me an amused look, "Like I said, you called me. Here I am. If you don't need me, send me back. Doesn't get more clear than that."

"*How* did I call you?" This was getting ridiculous. How would I send her back? Back where?

She just stared at me as if trying to tell if I was serious. Then gesturing, "The ring."

I looked down at my right hand. The ring from Elmer's box. I had put it on when I was going through the jewelry. I must have forgotten to take it off.

"I called you with . . . a ring?" There was a joke there somewhere, but my mind was still stuck on this woman standing in my bedroom. Talking to me like I was an idiot. Maybe I was going about this all wrong.

I sighed and tried again. "Listen. I'm kind of, um . . . new to all of this. I'm sorry to have bothered you. I really didn't mean to . . . call you. And, if you'll tell me how, I will gladly send you back to, um . . . Where are you from?" Oh my God, I sounded like a blathering fool. Good thing speaking was one of my strong points, right?

That stare again. Rosemary walked toward me, eyes narrowed. Her shrewd gaze took in my sleep mussed hair, seeming to pause at my gray streak before returning to my face. "How *exactly* did you come by that ring?"

"I-It was given to me," I backed up a step, but the bed blocked any further retreat. Not knowing what else to do, I yelled for help. "Elmer! Jake! Get up here!"

"Elmer? Elmer who?" she demanded.

"Jenkins," Elmer answered, appearing in the middle of the room, Jake at his side. "Who did you think, cousin?"

"Well, I'll be. You want to explain yourself, cousin? You have a woman on the other side missing you something fierce. What are you still doing here, Elmer?" Then Rosemary gestured at me. "And why is she wearing that? Without a clue in the world?"

Elmer looked lost for a moment at the mention of his wife. "I was kind of hoping you might be able to help her out. I wasn't positive the jewelry would even work for her."

I sat down heavily on the bed, watching them banter back and forth. Looking at the clock next to the bed, I realized I had been asleep for less than twenty minutes. Maybe if I lay back down, this would all just go away.

"What if the ring hadn't worked? Or worse, what if Grandmam would have been the one to answer her call?"

"If the ring hadn't worked, there wouldn't be a problem, now would there? And if Grandmam had been the one to answer, I would have been here, same as I am with you." Elmer's chin jutted out stubbornly.

I sensed a bit of rivalry between these two. If this kept up much longer, I was going to break for popcorn.

"That ring is for *family* Elmer, and she doesn't look like blood," Rosemary spat back, glaring at me.

"*Family*—left everything behind Rosemary," his voice breaking a little at that. "It was her, or no one at all."

I stood up again. "Excuse me. I *really* hate to break up this, er, reunion or whatever, but can we get back to the matter at hand here please?"

They both turned to me. Elmer looked sheepish and Rosemary looked, well, cranky enough to make me want to sit back down and wish I had remained quiet.

"What's done is done, I guess," she conceded finally. To me she said, "Let's get you sorted out," she paused, then addressed Elmer, "You don't go anywhere. We need to talk."

"Rosemary," Elmer said softly, "there really was nobody else. I was pretty sure Roxanne, here, would be able to do this. She's strong. Just look at her. And—she has the Sight."

I made an effort not to fidget during their combined attention. Rosemary's expression eased a bit. "Yes. I can see that."

"Will you help, then?" Elmer looked hopeful. "There's just too much I can't teach her about. Especially everything to do with the jewelry. That's always been passed down by the womenfolk, and right now there are none left to do that."

Another moment of silence passed. "Fine. Tell me how—this girl—came to be wearing that ring, and we'll work from there."

Elmer caught her up to speed fairly quickly. By the time he finished, Rosemary was looking at me much more thoughtfully. I saw her eye my hair again and it was all I could do not to reach up and tuck the gray streak behind my ear.

"Well, that's quite a story there, Roxanne. I . . . may have been a bit abrupt with you in the beginning. How about we start over?"

I nodded; fairly sure this was as close as I would come to getting an apology from this cranky old woman.

"So, let's see what else you have. I can feel them nearby," she said, looking around the room.

I raised my brows questioningly at Elmer. He winked back and nodded. Permission granted, I turned to the nightstand and lifted out the little box, opening it as I set it on the bed. Rosemary walked over and looked everything over intently. When she reached down and picked up the opal pendant, I nearly fainted.

"How are you able to do that?"

She grinned over at me, "It's different when we're called back than before we cross over."

Curious now, I asked—mostly because I was afraid to do so without her permission, "Is it okay if I touch you?"

"Sure."

Tentatively, I reached out to touch her arm. I gasped softly; she was—

"Boo!"

I screamed and fell back onto the bed, nearly knocking the box of jewelry off. Her hearty laugh reverberated through the room. Even Elmer had the nerve to chuckle. Jake joined in with a soft woof, tail wagging furiously.

"Seriously? That could've given me a heart attack! Do you even *know* what a rough month I've had!"

That just brought on more laughter from them both, though Elmer at least looked somewhat embarrassed by it. Jake groaned and flopped down onto the floor, head between his massive paws, his tail thumping silently.

"Great. I'm being laughed at by a ghost, his ghost dog, and—" I paused, my anger quickly forgotten. "What the heck are you? And why is it that I can touch you, but not Elmer?"

Rosemary shrugged her shoulders. "Like I said. It's different when you're called back through. I don't know why exactly. It just is."

"So, are you . . . alive?" She had felt warm to me. She had felt real.

"No. Absolutely not," she set the pendant back into the box and picked up the gold and silver ring. "I'm just a different kind of energy than what Elmer here is, I guess you would say," she explained, replacing the ring.

Glancing back at the clock again I announced, "We've got roughly twenty-five minutes before Sam will be home. Unless she gets stuck at work." I grabbed my phone to see if there were any messages. Nothing. "She hasn't messaged me about anything, so let's assume twenty-five minutes. Is there a crash course we can do here?"

"That is not how it is done, Roxanne," Rosemary said flatly. "Normally, the knowledge is passed down to daughters, granddaughters, or nieces. It can take years to learn."

Deadpanning back at her, "You may not have noticed, but I'm not exactly a spring chicken here. I don't have years to learn . . . whatever all of this is." I reached down under the bed to pull out the bookbag. Dumping them on the bed, I gestured at them. "Is there one of these that can help me out? Or at least give me a place to start?"

Rosemary trailed her fingers lightly over the covers, her eyes tearing. "These are generations of history, written by the women of my family. Most of them tell of local happenings. We used them to try to determine what areas seemed to draw what kind of Others and whether or not there were cycles we could determine." She sniffled a bit. I honestly didn't know if I should hand her a tissue or not. What were the rules of etiquette when dealing with a—not ghost? "And this," she said, picking up the older book. "This is the family Grimoire." I had no clue what that meant.

Clearing my throat, "What about the jewelry then? We can start with this," I held up my hand, ring facing forward.

"That ring is Rose Quartz. It has healing abilities, but it has to draw on some of your own energy. And it doesn't instantly heal a person—they'll just heal a lot faster than they would on their own. Also, as you've already found out, you can use it to call someone back through from the other side. Only temporarily, of course. As far as I know, it'll be someone from my family that answers—or at least that's how it's always been before. Nobody outside of the family has ever worn that ring before," she shot a look at Elmer. He studiously ignored her. She shook her head and continued, "This will also use some of your energy, so don't do it just for company. You are probably going to sleep pretty heavy tonight. I would take the ring off before you go to bed if I were you. It is supposed to have other abilities, but sometimes it works differently for different people. I can tell you what I know but, like I said, no one besides family has ever worn it before, so it might be different for you."

I pulled out the opal pendant she had first picked up. "What about this one?"

"That one was our family's spirit stone. It was made special for one of our ancestors," she leveled a stern look at Elmer. He looked back at her impassively. "It kept the wearer safe and invisible from certain kinds of Others. Not all of them, mind you. Witches, mostly. Possibly Vampires, but they don't seem to bother with us much anyway, for some reason. Grandmam used to say she could spirit walk with it."

"I think I might have one . . . kind of like it," I offered tentatively. "It belonged to my grandmother. I inherited it when my mother passed away."

"Have you ever worn it?"

"No, not really. She didn't either, so far as I can remember. I think I played with it when I was little. What little girl doesn't play dress-up with her mom's jewelry?"

"Hmm. And you don't remember anything else about it?"

"Um, no, I don't think so."

"Did you have any crazy dreams when you had it on? Any nightmares?" she was watching me keenly at this point.

I thought back. I did have really odd dreams sometimes as a child. And a lot of nightmares. But were they different than any other child had? I shrugged, "I don't recall anything out of the ordinary."

"Maybe it's just a regular piece of jewelry, then. Hard to say," she was still watching me closely enough to make me squirm a little.

Nervously, I looked at the clock again. Sam would be home in about five minutes. "As informative as all of this has been, you should probably go now. Thank you for everything, Rosemary."

"Oh, we're not done yet. I'll tell you how to send me back, but you'll need to know about the rest of what's in that box before you go wearing any of it. Except maybe this," she picked up the opal pendant. "Wear it when you have to go outside of this house but take it off as soon as you return. And this," picking up the plain, almost crude silver ring and showing it to me. "Wear this when you read the Grimoire and the journals. They're, well, I guess you could say they're magicked to prevent just anybody from understanding them. This ring will take care of that."

She paused for a moment to let all of that sink in. "Everything in here will exact a price from you, mostly in energy, so wear them only when you need to. You'll have to build up a tolerance, of sorts, to pay that price, understand?"

I nodded.

"Now, to send me back, just think about what you want. You want me to return to where I came from. As soon as that's done, you take that ring off and put it back in the box, hear? When you want me to come back, put it on and think of me. Sometimes that helps with getting the person you actually want, but not always. Meditating or relaxing helps, which is probably what happened this time, when you fell asleep. Now let's go. Are you ready?"

I nodded quickly. Closing my eyes—

"You don't need to close your eyes to think, do you?"

I opened one eye to glare at her. She laughed. Closing that eye again, I thought about her going back to her side of the . . . whatever. Or maybe wherever? For some reason the words that popped into my head were *go back from whence you came*. That made me snicker.

"She's gone, Roxanne. You can open your eyes now," Elmer provided helpfully.

Blowing out a breath, I relaxed, only now realizing how tense I had been. What if I hadn't been able to send her back? How would I explain her to Sam? Would Sam have even been able to see her? As these questions barreled through my head, I pulled the ring off and placed it back into the box, which in turn went back into the nightstand drawer.

I heard the garage door opening for Sam's car as I carefully put the journals back into the bag, tucking it under the bed again. Straightening back up, I looked over at Elmer, Jake still flopped lazily on the floor beside him. He smiled, waved, and they were both gone in a blink.

I headed down the stairs just as Sam was walking in. All through dinner I struggled with myself as to whether or not to tell my friend about any of this. Not to mention *how* to tell her. It all sounded crazy, even to me—and I was the one living it. I decided to wait a couple more days and broach it to Elmer, first. How had my life become so freaking weird? Oh yeah. Steven.

Chapter 9

I was just stepping out of the shower the next morning as my phone rang. I saw Sam's name pop up on the Caller I.D. and answered it.

"Hey, Rox. I wanted you to hear this from me first," she said right away.

I paused before answering. Perhaps it was just a gut feeling but I was pretty sure I knew why she was calling me this early.

"He's out, isn't he?" I asked, dread filling me.

"Yes, he is. There was nothing more I could do. He's already been detained far longer than normal. His lawyer has been petitioning pretty hard for his bail to be lowered. The judge finally allowed it—I don't think he had much choice. I was able to place a personal protection order as one of the conditions, though. He can't come near you."

"Where did he get the money from?" I knew we didn't have that much in our checking account. If he had somehow accessed our savings, wouldn't I have been notified?

"He put part of it on a credit card and the rest—from your joint savings."

"What? Can he do that?"

"He can," Sam said, apologetic. "You two always kept separate cards, right?"

We had, thank goodness. Mostly because I hardly ever used credit cards. The one I kept for emergencies only had a two-thousand-dollar limit. "Yes. But what about the savings? That's in both of our names. He can't just take that money, can he?" I scrambled for a towel, slipping on the floor a bit. I was trying hard not to hyperventilate.

"Have you taken any money out?"

"No, none. Why?"

"It can get tricky with divorce when one person tries to empty out joint accounts. The courts can force repayment—with interest. If you don't need the money for anything right now," she knew I didn't, "withdraw roughly half of what's left in all of your joint accounts. Set it up in a separate account—just don't touch it. Treat it like an escrow. Make sure you print out the last few months' worth of statements, too. As far as the money you inherited from your parent's estate? He has no rights to any of that."

I did already know most of this but hearing it from her helped push the panic away. Though Sam didn't specialize in divorce cases, she would still take them on in special circumstances—like mine—so she had kept up on current divorce law. Up until a few years ago, I had too.

"So, what now?" I asked as I quickly dried off and threw on a robe.

"Well, he can't come within three hundred feet of you, he can't call you or directly contact you in any way, and he can't purchase a firearm."

"Okay . . . how far away is my house from yours, would you say?"

"It's two hundred and seventy-five feet from my back door to the curb in front of your house," I could almost hear the grin in her voice. "If you can see him, he's violating the PPO and can go back to jail. Any arrangements to pick up his personal items from the house have to be made through his lawyer and myself. Also, are you sitting down?"

"I am now," as I curled my legs up onto one of the chairs in my room. "Is it that bad?"

"Nothing we can't handle, Rox, but—he wants to fight the divorce," she said. "He is insisting he will go for counseling himself and—he wants to do marriage counseling. He may try to block the sale of the house, too."

"No way! Absolutely not. No. Freaking. Way. You know how he is, Sam. He never lets anything go."

"I figured that would be your answer. I'll take care of the paperwork on our side of this. He can't force you—this is just a delay tactic. I've scheduled the first mediation hearing day for this Friday. I've got most of the preliminary paperwork already done and I want to move quickly. There will probably be two or possibly even three sessions, depending on how bullheaded he decides to be. The first will be just his lawyer and myself. If we're lucky, you'll only have to attend the final session, mostly to sign papers. Think you're ready for this?"

I felt like I was going to start hyperventilating again. I forced myself to take slower, deeper breaths.

"You okay, Rox?" Sam asked, concern in her voice.

"Yes. Yes, I'm fine. Just—trying not to panic. Um, if this is going to come down to negotiations I need something that's going to push his buttons. I was thinking—"

"The Camaro!" we both said in unison.

"He did acquire it after you were married so it is half yours, Roxie. Are the keys still over at the house?"

"Yes. They should be with my spare keys. I'll get them when I head over to the house. He does have the set he keeps with his truck keys, though. Know anyone with a boot?"

"I just might," she said thoughtfully. "Let me make a few calls. Oh, and I'm picking dinner up on the way home. How does Tia Helita's sound?"

"Fantabulous!" I loved Mexican food and she knew Tia Helita's was one of my favorites. She was trying to cheer me up. Best. Friend. Ever.

"The usual?" She always made fun of me because I generally ordered the same thing every time—seafood enchiladas with rice and beans.

"Of course."

After we said our goodbyes and hung up, I put my face in my hands. I wanted to just scream. Instead, I took a deep breath and blew it out slowly. I had Sam. I had my friends. And now I had some freaky Sight that allowed me to see things I never knew existed and a box full of jewelry that had—powers or whatever. I could do this. Right?

I quickly did my hair and the minimal makeup I bothered with—Sam didn't care what I looked like and it's not like we were expecting company. Who was I going to impress—Elmer?

Walking over to my nightstand drawer, I only hesitated for a moment before bringing out the wooden jewelry box and the journal detailing the drawings. Looking around the room for a space that would work best, I decided the bed would be the most comfortable.

My hips complained vehemently as I settled into a seated position with my legs crossed, Native American style. I tucked a pillow under my butt, and they quieted to a low grumble, barely heard over my knees creaking and popping every time I shifted my weight. Maybe I should have gone to those yoga classes with Sam, after all. In all fairness, I had gone to two sessions with her. I just never went back after I couldn't move for nearly three days after the second class. That had been a few years ago. Lately, she had started asking if I wanted to go with her on her morning runs but I had begged off with fairly flimsy excuses so far.

Opening the box, I took out the Rose Quartz ring, barely hesitating before slipping it on my finger. Closing my eyes, I worked to deepen my breathing and clear my mind. I pictured Rosemary's face in as much detail as possible.

I opened one eye and looked around the room. Nothing. Sighing, I tried again. Maybe deeper breaths would help. After less than thirty seconds of this, I started to get a little dizzy. Crap. I looked down at the ring on my right hand. It could be too soon. It had only been yesterday since I used it, after all. I took it back off and started to uncross my legs, when a charley horse grabbed a hold of my left calf. I tried not to scream as the pain spasmed through my leg. I jumped off of the bed faster than my body normally moved, desperately trying to straighten my leg muscles and stretch my calf before the pain hit excruciating. I didn't get these very often, but I knew I had to head it off at the pass, or else.

"Put the ring back on, you idiot," a voice bellowed right next to my ear.

I screamed and the muscle spasm deepened. Tears blurred my vision—I couldn't even see who was yelling at me. I felt someone pry my fisted hand open and slide the ring back onto my finger. My leg stopped cramping almost immediately.

"What the heck were you doing?" asked the voice I now recognized as Rosemary's.

"W-wait. I need to c-catch my b-breath," I gasped out, holding my hands up in a time-out sign. When I could finally breathe somewhat normally again, I wiped at my eyes and looked over at the gruff woman.

"Thanks," I said, still breathing rather shakily. "What the heck was that?"

"Looked like a leg cramp to me," she shrugged.

"Yeah, I got that part. Was it because I took the ring off?" I sat back down on the edge of the bed.

"No, of course not," she snorted. "That's a healing ring. It can't cause pain. Why do you think I told you to put it back on?"

"I thought maybe that was the price of using it. Or maybe it was too soon to use it again or something."

"Pish! Don't be stupid. It already took the energy it needed from you when you used it before."

"How am I supposed to know that? I'm the newb, here, remember?" I threw back at her.

Her brow wrinkled as she mouthed 'newb' to herself.

"I'm the newbie. New to all of—this," I explained, gesturing first at her, then the jewelry box.

She just eyed me curiously, glancing up at my hair again, before looking back down and shaking her head, "Well, I'm here now. What do you need?"

"I wanted to ask you some questions about the rest of the jewelry."

"Like what?"

"L-like what the rest of it does?"

"How long has it been?" she sighed.

"How long has it been since what?"

"Since you called me here," she said slowly, like I was a slow learner. At this rate, maybe I was. "You just said you thought maybe it was too soon."

"Oh, it was yesterday," I answered, feeling a bit foolish. How could she not know how long it had been. Were things that busy on the other side? "How long has it been for you?"

She had a full-on scowl at this point. "Time moves differently over there. It's not as—critical—for us, I guess you could say. Which doesn't mean you should be wasting it."

"Sorry! Really, I am. It's just that—my ex, er, almost ex, husband just got out of jail. And I know he's going to be angry. Are there any of these pieces of jewelry that could help with, like, protection? From a human instead of—you know?"

She studied me for a moment before replying with a question. "Is he the one that put you in the hospital?"

I nodded.

Her eyes softened a bit as she seemed to come to a decision. "There is one that might help some. And it won't take any energy unless it has to be used—just wearing it won't draw anything from you." She walked over to the bed and flipped open the little box. "Here," she plucked out another ring, this one with a black stone, and dropped it into my palm. She sat down next to me. "Wear this one. Its base power is protection. It should work against most anything normal, but it won't stop an all-out attack or a bullet, mind you. It works differently than that. I never wore this one, just heard it spoken of. I guess you could say if someone really wants to hurt you, when they draw close enough, they should lose some of that desire.

"The amount of energy it draws from you will depend on how hard it has to work to protect you. If someone's will to hurt you is strong enough to power past that ring, you might just pass out. And that wouldn't turn out so well for you, I'm sure. If you fear that happening, you take the ring off and slip it into your pocket or purse and you do what any smart person would do."

"What's that?"

"You run for help," she replied sternly. "There is never any shame in that. Being brave is for the really powerful or the really

87

stupid. Of course, there are those that fit into both of those categories, I'm sure."

"Thank you. I—this helps. Really," I said softly. "This whole world that I've been thrown into, that I never even knew existed, is just a lot to take in, you know?"

She laughed, smiling a little. I was amazed at how much it changed her whole face. She looked pretty, almost—handsome—I think is the term they used to use to describe women like her.

"Honey, this world is a lot to take in even when you do grow up knowing about it. Heck, it might even be worse, knowing."

She might have a point there.

"Well, do you want me to send you back now?" I asked. After her comment about time working differently there and not wasting it, I didn't want to keep her any longer than necessary.

"Is that all you needed?" she asked. She almost sounded friendly.

"Yes. For now anyway. I'll, um, I'll try not to bother you anymore than I have to. I was just really freaked out today. Again, thank you."

Nodding, she stood up. "Good. Tonight's poker night and the dealer is what I think you all call a 'hottie', these days."

Now it was my turn to laugh. I closed my eyes and sent her back. I took the Rose Quartz ring off and put it back into the jewelry box. Hesitating only a second, I slipped the ring Rosemary had pulled out on the ring finger of my right hand. Weirdly enough, just like the other ring, this one fit perfectly. I shook my head.

Maybe it was magick.

Chapter 10

The next day . . .

I can do this. If I keep repeating that enough, maybe I'll actually believe it.

Stepping foot back into my house, my home, shouldn't have been this difficult. I had already deactivated the security alarm. Closing my eyes, I took a deep breath and turned the key to unlock the front door. My Jeep was still in the driveway, where it had sat since that fateful day. I'd always parked in the driveway, considering Steven's truck and classic Camaro hogged all of the garage space. Or they had, anyway. I peeked in through the garage's side door on my way through the side yard and noted the truck was gone. I didn't know where it was, nor did I care.

Done stalling, I gave the door a push and stepped inside the house. Mentally, I couldn't call it home anymore. The air was a bit stale but, other than that, everything looked exactly the same. I don't know why I expected it to be different.

Walking without direction, I stopped at the sliding doors. The screen door still lay off to one side, where it had fallen when Steven—shaking my head, I quickly turned away. I would deal with that later. I knew the pool must be a mess—the stupid thing had to be cleaned constantly—but I just couldn't walk out there yet. My jaw began to ache just thinking about it, even though all of the external hardware had been removed a week ago.

I passed through the kitchen, taking mental notes of what needed to be done. There was a thin layer of dust on everything. The little pots of fresh herbs above the sink were well beyond the point of no return, shriveled and completely dried out. My mother would have rolled in her grave over the sight. Newly formed cobwebs in several corners meant dealing with those little freeloaders. Spiders had always been Steven's area. I wasn't afraid of them, but I didn't like them, either. My eyes roamed around the rest of the room, landing on the refrigerator. Ugh. I knew it had to be bad in there after over a month. The milk had been borderline iffy before I . . .

Maybe I'm not ready for this after all. I might be able to hire someone to come in and do all of the cleaning stuff and I can handle sorting and packing after.

I jumped, squeaked out a pitiful noise that might have been a scream, and had to clench tightly, or I would have peed my pants when my cell phone rang. One hand to my chest, like it was actually going to keep my heart from escaping, I fumbled through my purse for the phone with my other hand. It was Sam.

"Hey girl! How's it going?" her cheerful voice echoing through the too-quiet house.

"It's—weird. And kind of creepy."

"Nothing should be disturbed in there. I asked the police to do extra patrols for the first couple weeks to discourage anyone else from bothering anything there. I may have also mentioned to the Delaney's across the street that Michelle was persona non grata, right now. They promised to call the police or myself if they saw anything. And you *know* they see everything." Yeah, sometimes nosy neighbors could be a blessing. They meant well; I knew. "And when you were still in the hospital, I had an extra security camera added to the back of my house that covers most of the back of yours, too."

"That was probably smart, considering our gate." We had added that gate between our yards shortly after having the house built and were fencing for the pool. Steven hadn't been too much of a butthead about it, especially since Sam had insisted on paying for it. Because I was the only one that really used it, we had never even put a lock on it. "Sam, I don't know if I'm ready for this."

Silence. Then, "Hang on for a sec, 'kay?"

She must have muted the phone because there was nothing. I wandered into the dining room and then through to the living room.

She was back as suddenly as she'd gone. "Tell you what. Grab what you need for now out of the house. Pack whatever clothes you know you want; grab anything you think is important. If you're comfortable enough getting some of Steven's clothes and personal items together, that would be great. If not, we can arrange for him to be supervised and get what he needs himself. Anyway, I'll talk to you when I get home tonight. I've got an idea."

"Um, okay."

"Oh, and don't forget to change the security code on the alarm before you go, too, unless you want to keep the temporary one I programmed in. See you later. Call me if you need anything," and she was gone.

Tucking my phone back in the purse, I looked upstairs. If being this jumpy was my new normal—and considering the gift I now had thanks to Steven's fist, it was—I might have to start wearing panty liners full time! Forty going on forty-one was not being kind to my bladder. Maybe it was a good thing I hadn't had children, after all. I started up the stairs to our bedroom, thinking back to the events that had led to all of this and trying to pinpoint when everything had started to go so wrong.

When Steven and I first met, it felt like we were always on the same page. We were both at the point in our lives where we were ready for—more, I guess. Marriage, kids, a big house—the works. Soon after we were married, we casually began trying to have a baby, celebrating by throwing my birth control pills away. It didn't happen right away, but we weren't overly worried, figuring it would happen when it happened. Steven had Michelle from a previous marriage, but he insisted he wanted at least one more. At that time, Michelle wasn't nearly the terror she grew up to be. She was aloof and moody, something I put down to her just being a normal teenager. The idea of a ready-made family didn't bother me, I had liked the idea at the time. I'd tried everything I could think of to bond with her in the beginning—taking her out shopping and having 'just us girls' nights. When we had this house built, I made a big deal out of her new room and encouraged her to decorate it in her own style, offering to help her pick out colors, furnishings, whatever she wanted. I never received so much as a thank you from that girl—or from Steven for that matter. She had Steven wrapped around her little finger and she knew it. When it finally became apparent that we would never have any children of our own, Steven had grown more and more distant. He spoiled Michelle, heaping his attention on her, never even correcting her when she treated me rudely.

I sighed as I walked into the bedroom and looked around. As I did, I realized I hated it. It was a nice enough room; the furniture was all quality dark woods and it all matched. But it was boring. The walls were beige, just like the rest of the house. Neutral. Whenever I suggested something to give any of the rooms a pop of color or a bit of life, Steven shot the idea down without even considering it. I learned early on that he was either intimidated by color or just plain didn't like it. He would never allow it to be open for discussion, either. His stupid reasoning 'it would be better for resale' was just that. Stupid. This house had supposedly been our dream so why would we sell?

That thought stopped me mid step. It would be sold now. Unless Steven bought me out of my half. I had put nearly all of my savings, which had been substantial, into this house. Steven made good money, but his first divorce had really set him back financially. And, of course, there were the child support payments that took nearly a quarter of his pay until Michelle finally turned eighteen. Then there was college tuition and *expenses*—she'd refused to get a job through either high school or college, of course. I wasn't so sure he *would* be able to afford to keep the house. There was no way I wanted to keep it, even if I could afford it. I had what was left of the moderate inheritance from my parents tucked away in savings but that was it. Plus, I had no real job anymore. The odds and ends stuff I did for Sam's firm now was fun money, at best.

How did my life become so messed up?

I quickly grabbed what I needed out of my dresser, including the spare set of keys I had tucked away, and threw it into a small duffel. I just wanted to grab my mom's jewelry, a few pairs of my own jeans, some sweats and t-shirts—I had lost weight, but Sam's were still more than a bit snug on me—and get out of here. I went into the walk-in closet and stopped dead in my tracks. The door to the safe in the corner was slightly ajar. Stooping down, I opened it and looked inside. We kept some cash, the gun Steven insisted we have for personal protection, the jewelry my mother had left me plus some of my own that was somewhat valuable, and copies of most of our legal documents in here. Except for some of the papers, it was pretty much emptied. I sat down hard, stunned. *Had Steven taken everything? Or had Michelle snuck back in without being noticed, somehow?* And then, *the pendant! Crap!*

I reached in for the papers and my hand felt something sandwiched between some of them. As I pulled them out a ring fell to the floor. I held it up, not recognizing it as one that I had ever purchased. It must have fallen out of the envelope containing the jewelry from my mother. I slipped it on the finger of my left hand, gathered up the rest of the loose papers, and looked inside one more time to make sure I hadn't missed anything. It was completely empty.

I quickly closed the safe door, not bothering to lock it—what was the use? Grabbing the clothes I needed, I left the house as fast as I could manage, barely remembering to reprogram the security system on my way out. Steven could get whatever he needed, himself. Under supervision. He would hate every minute of that. *Serves him right!* Instead of walking back the way I had come, I decided to drive my Jeep back to Sam's.

***

I walked in, looking around for Elmer and Jake. I called out for them softly. Nothing. Not really feeling up to another lesson today anyway, I went up to my room. My mind kept cycling back to the safe, trying to remember exactly what had been in there. The loose papers I had brought with me turned out to be miscellaneous receipts and the warranties for appliances we had purchased. Grabbing a pen and one of my notepads, I sat down and closed my eyes, thinking.

The gun. Of course, that *would* be at the forefront. I shuddered, not wanting to imagine how things would have turned out if Steven had grabbed that gun before confronting— no, *assaulting*—me by the pool. Maybe I would be safe here, hanging out with Elmer and Jake, just ghosting it up. I snorted at that. *Focus.* Hmm. There were copies of our marriage license, birth certificates, social security cards, titles to our vehicles—all the usual documents. The originals were in a safety deposit box at our credit union. My parent's death certificates were in there. I think there was around seven hundred in cash, but it had been months since either of us had taken any money out or put it back in, so I was just guessing. It was emergency money, more than anything. The small box of jewelry with a few nicer pieces that Steven had bought me early on in our marriage and some that I had before we were married. The rest of the jewelry was my mother's. Being an only child, I inherited everything when they passed three years ago. Their wedding rings had been in a little envelope, along with several more valuable looking rings, chains, and such—all of which had been tucked into a larger padded envelope. And I was positive the pendant I remembered had been in with all of it. I had planned to have the whole lot appraised someday but had simply never gotten around to it. I regretted that now. The ring on my hand was all I had left. Glancing at it, I decided to take it off, tucking it away into the little wooden box with Elmer's jewelry for now.

Turning my attention back to the list I had made, I sighed. I was probably wasting my time doing this. I would ask Sam about my chances of getting any of it back when she came home.

For the next two hours I busied myself with putting the things I'd brought back with me away, laundering the clothes Sam had loaned me, and puttering around the kitchen and trying to decide what to make for dinner.

Mostly, I was trying not to think about the missing contents of the safe.

Chapter 11

At a loss for what else to do until Sam came home that evening, I grabbed a broom and started for the attic stairs. I only hesitated for a moment before heading up, broom in front of me to brush away the cobwebs. I was proud to realize I wasn't even slightly out of breath by the time I got to the top of the steep staircase.

Looking over at all of the totes and boxes stacked at the end of the room, I remembered how sad Elmer had looked, knowing his children didn't want any of this stuff. When my parents had passed, it had been incredibly difficult for me to get rid of anything at all. In the end I kept everything that had any sentimental value and made sure that anything I couldn't keep was donated and would help somebody else. Clothing, furniture, and household items went to the Salvation Army and several area women's shelters. My dad's older model car had been in excellent condition—that went to a Habitat for Humanity charity auction. Steven had nearly lost it when he found out how much I had donated instead of selling everything for the money. *Served him right for leaving me to take care of all of it on my own. He hadn't wanted to be bothered dealing with any of it, so he didn't have any say in it.* I knew I had done the right thing. My parents would have been happy with how I handled it all, I was positive.

I walked over to the first stack of totes. Several were labeled glassware. The top box on the next stack was just labeled 'dining room'. I looked over the next few totes and they just had general labels, such as 'kitchen', 'china', or 'books'. I paused at one of the several that was labeled 'books'. Sam's house had a small parlor with built-in bookshelves. We had joked that maybe it had been a library for the previous owners. She ended up filling one entire shelf, top to bottom, with the law books she collected. The rest of the shelves she used more for display cases for little things. She had joked about filling them up with books someday. Hmmm.

I moved back to the boxes of glassware. I tested the weight of the top box, just to make sure I would be able to lift it without dropping it. It was manageable, but only barely. I set it down carefully and took the lid off. Everything inside was protectively wrapped in newspaper. Kneeling down, I unwrapped one of the items on the top and gasped. Elmer had been right. I held up the dainty pink glass teacup to the light. The patterns in the glass were gorgeous. I rewrapped the cup and checked a few of the others. They were all the same. Pink Depression Glass teacups. As heavy as this box had been, there must be a complete set in it.

Closing the box back up, I gently pushed it aside and stood. The boxes were only stacked two or three high along the wall. This stack was one that had three boxes. The next box I left in place so I wouldn't have to kneel down to open it and listen to my knees complain. I undid the top and took out the first thing on top, again unwrapping it carefully. It was a small mixing bowl. Looking back in the box, I saw it had been inside what was probably the next size larger bowl. It was bright yellow and looked practically new. I checked the bottom. Pyrex. *I can't believe that none of his children wanted any of this. These are beautiful. And probably valuable!* I rewrapped the little bowl and nested it back in the other bowl. Blowing my hair out of my face, I looked back down the stack of totes. Maybe Sam and I should go through all of this together. I knew she wouldn't be upset that I was up here snooping, especially since she didn't even know what was up here, but technically this was all hers now.

I closed the box up and put the first box back in place. Maybe I should ask Elmer about this stuff one more time before I brought it up to Sam. There had to be a reason his children had left it behind—it just seemed unlikely it was just forgotten.

I headed back down the stairs to my room, where I grabbed my laptop and ran a search for Eleanor Jenkins. Several dozen popped up in this area. The first eight were death records. What if his youngest daughter was dead? That thought gave me pause—wouldn't he know if she had died, somehow? I had no idea how all of that worked. Realizing this brought something else to the forefront of my mind.

Growing up, my family had gone to church, though not always regularly. We still found ways to worship even when we didn't attend. The three of us volunteered at soup kitchens, homeless shelters, retirement homes, and other charitable causes on a regular basis. My parents donated to those places as well, instead of tithing to the church. My mother believed that the 'Powers That Be', as she called them, would rather we put our money where our mouth was and be out doing good things in the world, not sitting in a church singing songs and listening to sermons about what was wrong with the world.

Steven didn't attend church at all. We were married in a church that had been converted over to a wedding chapel, but I hadn't really thought much of it at the time. Friends and family were all there with us, so that was what mattered most to me. Since then, I still made it a point to volunteer regularly, and donated regularly to various charities, but I had only attended church a handful of times. Steven insisted people only went to church to network their business, to show off what they had, or to gossip about others in the guise of being religious. It became easier to not go at all instead of listening to his version of a sermon every time I did.

Now, with everything I had experienced in the last few days, I wasn't even sure what to believe anymore. I actually felt a little— lost. Was the place that Elmer referred to and that Rosemary could be pulled back from—Heaven? Was it something else? Would Rosemary know if Eleanor was still alive or not?

I almost grabbed the Rose Quartz ring and called for her. As I started to open the drawer, I thought better of it, slowly pushing it closed again. I had already brought her over twice in the past two days. I don't know if she would appreciate seeing me again so soon. Heck, I wasn't sure what I would even ask her. *Hey Rosemary? How's Heaven? What's it like over there? Do you ever get to hang with The Big Guy?* Did I even want to know those answers?

As I started to close my laptop, an idea occurred to me. I wondered what the internet would have about magick, ghosts, magickal rings, witches, vampires, and the Sight. I opened it back up and started digging.

Within half an hour, I realized it was useless. I had tried different wordings with Google on each topic and had come up with all sorts of books, movies, and games. I had even searched 'ghost dog'. Apparently, that was a really popular nineties movie. Oh, and I learned that Weimaraners were also known as ghost dogs. Now I had ads that kept popping up for movies, dogs, psychics, anointing oils, jewelry, as well as various historical references for witches and vampires—many conflicting. None of it was even remotely close to what I had learned from Elmer or Rosemary. *This is impossible!*

I gave up and flopped back on the bed, groaning as I noted the time on the clock. Sam wasn't due home for another two hours. Realizing I hadn't eaten lunch, I decided to find something to snack on before dinner. With the weight I had lost from my jaw injury—and was still continuing to lose from what Sam called the 'divorce diet'—my waistline could afford snacks these days. I'm not sure if the price was worth it, though.

Downstairs, I quickly threw together a plate of cheese cubes, grapes and crackers, then headed back up to my room.

As I ate, the journal with depictions of the jewelry in the box came to mind. I pulled the book bag out from under the bed. I opened the drawer in the bedside table and lifted out the small wooden box and it's matching little picture journal, setting them beside me on the bed as I arranged my pillows behind me to sit up to read.

The little silver ring looked way too small for any of my fingers as I picked it up, turning it every which way as I examined it. I don't know why, but I tried it on the tip of my pinkie finger. There was no way it was going to fit—but it slid on perfectly. Almost as if it had sized itself. I wasn't sure if it was my imagination or what, but I thought I saw it shimmer once as it slid into place. When I blinked and looked again, it seemed somewhat more stylish than it had been in my hands. Huh!

Picking up the smaller book with the drawings, I opened the cover and my breath caught. I could hardly believe what I was seeing. The picture that had originally looked hand-drawn now looked *so real* I had to do a double-take to make sure I had the right journal in my hands. I did. The semi-washed out, amateurish charcoal illustrations were gone. These looked more like 3-D computer renderings that you could reach out and pluck from the page. And the text—it was now very neatly arranged. There were perfectly legible descriptions of each piece, with details such as what it was made of, who made it, when it was made, as well as who charmed it and when. There were even examples of what its main use was, as well as minor uses or benefits—and most importantly, *how* to make it work. For every piece. I was stunned.

As a test—I took the ring off while staring at a picture. It immediately reverted back to the almost indecipherable mess it had been before. I put it back on—and it cleared right up. I stared at the little ring in amazement and blew out a shaky breath. It was like a decoder ring. This had been my first real taste of magic, or magick as Rosemary called it, and I think my mind was officially blown! Wasn't that what all the cool kids said these days? Ha! Maybe I didn't need reading glasses after all.

I continued flipping through the pages, not really paying attention to all of the individual details. There were only perhaps a dozen illustrations, I noted, while the rest of the pages were completely blank. I flipped backwards slowly through the little book until I reached the last page with a drawing on it—and nearly dropped the book.

I scrambled for the jewelry box, nearly knocking it off the bed in my haste. Setting it on top of the journal to hold the page, I rooted through for the ring I had dropped in there just this morning. Spotting it, I held it up to the light from the window. The center oval gem, clear stone, crystal, or whatever it was sparkled almost as brightly as a diamond. I doubted it was an actual diamond, though I wasn't sure what made me believe that. There were six smaller faceted gems or crystals set evenly around the main stone, in varying colors. The silver band didn't have any etchings like Elmer's jewelry did, it was very plain. Overall, it was a rather pretty ring, but not something I would have purchased for myself. I placed the ring on the page next to the illustration. They looked identical!

I read the description under the picture. *Ring of Power. The Clear Quartz Crystal focal point amplifies energy and intentions. Used for healing and protection on many different levels as long as the support stones are intact. The support stones power the focal crystal and will not draw energy from the wearer unless severely damaged. The Ring of Power will enhance other Items of Power when worn together and can be used to charge or power them, as well. The ring must be cleansed and recharged for a new wearer. To use: focus, intent, and strength of will are key. Maker: unknown. History: unknown.*

Stunned, I didn't know what to think. Picking the ring up and examining it again I wondered how on earth a ring from my safe could be in a journal that belonged to Elmer's family? And how the heck did you recharge a ring? I think I had a jewelry cleaning kit at home, but I wasn't going back there by myself anytime soon. I always used to clean my wedding ring at the kitchen sink with either Dawn dish soap or baking soda and an old toothbrush, so maybe that would work on this ring, too.

I looked over at my laptop again. Google hadn't been all that helpful so far, but I was willing to give it another chance. As I turned it back on, I noted the time. Sam should be home soon. Where had the afternoon gone?

I searched Quartz Crystal cleaning and recharging. Over a dozen sites and links popped up. I scrolled down looking for whichever one seemed the most promising, hoping for one without clickbait. I clicked on one partway down the page when I saw 'cleansing and recharging your crystals' in the lead description. After agreeing that yes, I knew the site used cookies, etc. and closing three pop-ups that wanted my email address so that I could be signed up for their newsletter or offering me discounts on my purchase today, I finally got to the article. Frowning as I read through it, I exited the site and went to another one, repeating the same process I had on the first. Did people really believe this stuff? I looked at the ring again. What the heck, it's not like I had anything to lose. Going through the steps each site described wasn't any crazier than talking to ghosts or reading magickal journals about magickal jewelry, right?

Needing to process everything that had happened today, I tucked everything away again, including my Power Ring, or whatever it was. I hurried downstairs and started setting out the antipasto salad I had prepared earlier, along with fruit and the crusty bread Sam favored. I had just grabbed a bottle of wine and two glasses, when she walked in.

Looking over the spread on the snack bar, where we usually ate dinner, she laughed. "Honey, I'm home. You know, Roxie, I could totally get used to this."

"It's the least I could do. I know I should probably go to my house, but—I just can't. Not yet, anyway."

"We've talked about this. You don't need to go anywhere, right now. Let me go change really quick before we eat," she said, already heading for the stairs.

"Sure, no problem." I opened the bottle of wine and filled our glasses, then sat down to wait. Looking around, I realized I hadn't seen Elmer all day. I wondered if he was expecting me to learn everything from Rosemary now or if he would continue my lessons, too.

Through most of dinner, we made small talk. Knowing how she was going to react, I waited until we were nearly done before telling her about the safe.

"That A-hole! I'll see if I can get a manifest of what he had on his person when he was taken in. The gun? That's huge. Neither of you ever got your concealed carry permit, right?"

I reached for another piece of bread, tearing off small bites, mostly to give my hands something to do. "No. It was one of those things we were going to do but just hadn't gotten around to."

"He won't be getting that back, then, not without a fight and cutting through a lot of red tape. Not when he was caught carrying without a permit right after assaulting you. Even that hotshot lawyer he hired won't be able to fight that."

Relief flooded me. "I still have to go to the bank and take care of the joint accounts. I hate this."

"Like I said before, just don't do anything crazy like empty them unless you set up an escrow account for the money. You know how it will work through the divorce proceedings."

I did. I just never thought I would be applying that knowledge to myself one day. At least all of our bills were on autopay. There was enough in our main account to handle several months' worth before I needed to worry unless Steven drained it.

Luckily, I kept the money I inherited from my parents estate in a separate account just in my name. I had used a large chunk of it to buy my Jeep Wrangler. Steven had grumped about that account and my 'selfish' purchase for close to a year. There wasn't a huge amount left, but it would be enough to carry me through the rough times I knew were ahead.

I snapped out of my musings when Sam tapped my arm.

"Sorry. What'd I miss?"

"I was asking what your plans were for next weekend. Where did you go?" she motioned to my head.

"Just . . . trying to figure everything out. Bills. The accounts. What happened. You know—everything."

"Rox, you are going to come out of all of this just fine. Better than just fine, even. How many times do I have to remind you who your lawyer is?"

I nodded absently. She was the best. I did know that.

I could tell she was itching to tell me something more but she waited until we were cleaning up before speaking what was on her mind.

"Before you object to what I'm going to say, please just hear me out. After talking to you this morning I started thinking maybe it would be easier if you had some help over at the house. Tess agrees. We both freed up our schedules for next weekend so we can be there with you to get everything cleaned and packed up. We'll take pictures of all of it, of course, before and after shots, for any legal reasons that may come up. Oh, and I've also talked to Annie, she's going to do all of the big cleaning. She even offered to help with any painting, if it needs touch ups or whatever. She's excited to help."

Annie had been Sam's housekeeper since before she renovated this house, having cleaned for her back when Sam leased a loft downtown near the office. She was only a few years younger than we were and was not only a hard worker, but she often kept us in stitches with her stories. The woman was a serious man-hater and we loved it. We had adopted her into our group immediately. Tess had been inducted shortly after.

"What? I'll pay her. I'm grateful for the help, but I know she could use the money." Annie was a single mother with a special needs child.

Sam lifted her brow at me. "You want to argue it out with her?"

Definitely not. The woman was both proud and fierce. She might be tiny, but she could take me in an unfair fight. I knew she fought dirty.

"I'll make it up to her somehow," I conceded. And I would, even if it meant slipping cash into her purse or dropping groceries off at her home.

I wasn't the least bit surprised at everyone's willingness to help. The four of us had been there for each other through several major crises. It wasn't that long ago that we had all rolled up our sleeves and moved Tess from her apartment into a house. It still made me tear up, though. After the crazy last couple of weeks I'd had, I really wished I could share everything with them. Or even just Sam.

Chapter 12

Before I headed up for bed, I grabbed a glass of water from the fridge. It was purified water, run through a reverse osmosis system, so I figured it should be okay to use tonight. Sam had already gone up to her room and would be up preparing for whatever was on her docket tomorrow morning. Opening the sliding glass door to the deck, I looked up to check the moon. It was a fairly clear night and the nearly full moon hung low in the sky. I sat the glass on one of the little tables that sat to one side of the door and stepped back inside quickly, relocking the slider behind me. I felt a little foolish doing this, but here I was. What was the saying? If I read it on the internet, it must be true?

As I reached the bottom of the stairs, I looked around one last time for Elmer. Should I be worried about him? He had been in a funk since seeing Rosemary. If she was willing to help me with learning what I needed to know to survive with my new 'abilities', maybe he should really start thinking about going to be with Birdie. I made a mental note to talk to him about it.

By the time I finished my nighttime routine and finally climbed into bed, I was so tired I was positive I would fall asleep before my head hit the pillow. Surprisingly, even with the insanity I had experienced since coming home from the hospital, I hadn't had any nightmares since regaining my memory of

Steven's assault. I usually slept like the dead, except for the twice a night trips to the bathroom because my bladder seemed to be shrinking with age. I grimaced. Perhaps 'like the dead' wasn't the best analogy. With that thought I drifted off.

The next morning, I woke earlier than normal. I could hear Sam getting ready to leave. I thought about staying in bed, but my morning bladder was worse than my midnight bladder. I got up and took my time getting ready, so as to stay out of Sam's way. She wasn't a breakfast person—or a morning person, for that matter—or I would have been only too happy to have it ready for her before she left. Goodness knows I had done it for Steven for the better part of a decade, even when I still worked full time.

When I finally heard the garage door close, I grabbed the Power Ring, as I now called it in my head, and went downstairs. I almost didn't make it past the coffee pot, but I told myself this would only take a minute, and the coffee would still be there when this task was done. Once again, Elmer was nowhere to be seen. As I opened the door to the back deck, I noted he wasn't sitting out there, either. Seeing the glass sitting on the side table made me pause. Had the water sat long enough under the moon? Would this even work? For that matter, would I even know if it worked?

Rolling my eyes, I picked up the glass, dropping the ring into it. Holding it up, I looked at the ring. It didn't look any different. Neither of the articles had mentioned *how long* the cleansing took. Or maybe I hadn't read enough of the articles to get to that part. Bringing the glass—with the ring still in it—back inside, I sat it on the counter while I fixed my coffee, adding a generous amount of creamer.

"What are you doing?"

I squeaked and jumped, nearly spilling my coffee. "Annie! What is it with everyone trying to scare the living daylights out of me?"

"Who else has been scaring you? It can't be Sam—you can hear her coming from a mile away. I think she starts talking before she even enters a room," the tiny brunette asked, amused. Her trademark snarky t-shirt read 'I'm actually not funny—I'm just mean, and people think I'm joking'. She came over and hugged me. "How are you feeling?"

"Er, no one. I'm feeling better, thanks. It's just—" I stammered, hugging her back. "I've been overly jumpy lately, I guess. And I thought I was alone. Didn't I hear the garage door shut already?" I thought for a second. "Hey, don't you normally come over earlier in the week?"

"Sorry. I really didn't mean to scare you. It's not like you don't have good reason, right? That was me shutting the garage door after I came in. I got here just before Sam left but I was trying not to wake you," she explained. "I had to switch my days this week because of Cammie's physical therapy schedule."

"Oh, is everything okay?" I asked, immediately concerned. Cammie, Annie's daughter, had cerebral palsy. It was a mild form but still required regular physical therapy.

"Yes, she's fine. Her regular therapist is out right now, so she'll be working with a substitute for a while, is all. She said to say hello and that she hopes you are feeling better, by the way. That hug was from her, too." She looked at the glass on the counter curiously, then back at me. "So, what's this?"

Crap. How was I supposed to explain that I was recharging a crystal ring in water that had sat out under the moon overnight? "Um, that. I read something about soaking some types of crystals and gems. The ring has been sitting in my safe for a long time so I didn't know if it would get brittle or anything. You know, like crystal ware has to be soaked every so often?"

She nodded slowly, "I remember my mom used to soak her crystal in water with a little vinegar. She said that the vinegar would restore shine. I don't think I've ever heard about doing that with jewelry, though. And I don't know if it would affect the metal band. Probably depends on the metal."

"Oh, well, I just figured it wouldn't hurt." Hoping it had been in the water long enough, I dumped the glass in the sink, catching the ring deftly as it dropped out. I slid the ring on my left ring finger, where my wedding band used to reside. "Do you want any help?"

"What? No, I'm good, thanks. Hey, that ring is gorgeous!"

Annie had too much pride to let anyone who wasn't an employee help her, but she was always the first to be there for anybody else. Sam had convinced her several years ago to start her own cleaning company. It was small, but it had made a huge difference in her income. The biggest benefit was how much more time she now had for her daughter, though. She could have had one of her employees clean Sam's house, but Annie continued doing it herself.

"Thanks. It was my mom's. Or my grandma's maybe. I'm not exactly sure. How about a cup of coffee? It's still hot."

"That sounds great. Let me just go get started and then we'll talk more over a cup." She headed through to the laundry room.

In addition to managing the housekeeping and general household shopping, she also handled all of Sam's laundry, even the dry-cleaning drop-offs. Sam called Annie her off-site household manager and would be lost without her.

A few minutes later, she joined me again and we caught up over coffee. We both commiserated over men—her experience with her ex-husband had been as bad as mine. Worse, really, when I considered Cammie, too. His abuse was to blame for Cammie's cerebral palsy. He had admitted to becoming frustrated and shaking her to try to get her to stop crying while Annie was at work. He had often been verbally abusive toward Annie herself, but had never gotten physical and she'd never thought he would hurt his own child. She was brave enough to divorce him after that and was awarded full custody. Her whole life revolved around her daughter now. Since then she had become a card-carrying member of the man-hater's club. We often joked that she would be handing out flyers and holding meetings soon. Her typical response was that all women's problems start with men—menstruation, menopause, and mental breakdowns. Not necessarily in that order. She usually followed that up with saying that if she ever ran into her ex again, it had better be with her car at 60 mph or faster. And that she was glad she had Sam as a friend and a lawyer. She could keep us in stitches for days.

When she needed to head back to the laundry and get started on the rest of the house, I excused myself to go back up to my room. I wanted to see if I could find any reference to the jewelry in some of the other journals.

I started with the journals first, after putting on the ring that I decided I would officially refer to as the decoder ring in an effort to make this feel more normal and less . . . not normal. Flipping through the first one, not actually taking time to read the details of each event, I noted how casually everything was written. It was almost as if reporting about supernatural beings, or 'Others' as they were referred to in most of the journals, was on par with what happened on any regular day for most people.

Dear Diary, I saw a vampire today at the market. Oh, and I think Carla Sue has a new recipe for strawberry rhubarb pie.

I groaned. Were jokes really the way to get through this? How was this my life now? Oh yeah. Steven. And maybe genetics.

A page recounting a witch sighting caught my eye. It happened nearly sixty years ago, according to the date next to the entry. As I opened the journal up fully, my thumb brushed the date and my bedroom disappeared.

I looked around, not recognizing my surroundings. Glancing down at my feet, I saw I was still in my socks. Great. No shoes. Oddly enough my feet weren't cold.

Seriously? This is what goes through my mind when I'm—

That thought was interrupted when I noticed a young woman's face peek around from behind a huge tree. I studied her for a second, thinking it was odd she didn't notice me. And that she seemed rather familiar. Frowning, I followed her gaze over to a building—a parsonage I think it was called. A woman had just walked out of the building and was making her way down the steps. She looked around and then started walking in my direction.

I froze. Should I hide? I looked around, noticing the headstones. A cemetery? I took a casual step toward one of the larger stones, thinking I could either duck behind it or try to look like a grieving relative. In my socks. Ugh. Yeah, I should hide.

Ducking behind the headstone, I watched. The woman wasn't paying any attention to me at all. In fact, neither of the women were. The first one had pulled back around her tree, staying out of sight, but still trying to observe the newcomer. I stiffened as the second woman got closer and I was able to get a better look at her. Her features were . . . skewed and kind of fuzzy around the edges. It almost looked like her face was a mask, just not a very good one. She started to pass between the tree the girl was behind and my hiding spot, when she stopped abruptly. What was she doing? Was she sniffing the air? From my angle I could just barely see the young woman. She looked scared.

The second—I wasn't sure what to call her now. Not a person, for sure. Was she Other? Suddenly, it clicked, and I knew. She was a witch. She looked straight at the tree hiding the young woman and her expression changed. She looked excited and . . . predatory. As she took a slow step toward the tree, I looked all around me. There was a small branch that had fallen next to the headstone. I went to grab for it but my hand passed right through. Crap. I quickly stood up. I could see the full-blown panic on her face as she looked around for somewhere to run.

"Hey!" I yelled. The girl didn't react to my voice, but the witch's head snapped back in my direction. Her eyes scanned the area, passing right over me. What? Could she not see me? The young woman took that opportunity to sprint toward a car parked a couple hundred feet away in the small parking lot next to the building. The witch crouched and turned her attention back to her prey. I could almost see her gathering herself to chase her prey.

Heck, if she couldn't see me anyway, what did I have to lose, right? I took a step toward the witch and yelled again. "No!"

She started and spun back toward me again, perplexion written clearly on her face. She sniffed the air once more and then, still not seeing me, turned back, leaping forward to chase the girl again. The girl herself was really hauling butt, making good time getting away. If I could just stall the witch for a little longer, I think she might just make it.

"I. Said. No!" I yelled, bringing my hands up this time. I don't know what made me do it or how to explain what I did. I only knew I needed to do something.

One second the witch was moving, facing away from me and running after the girl, the next she was sprawled on the ground. She jumped up and whirled, looking in every direction around her, a snarl on her already distorted features. Perhaps non-features might have been a better description, I thought, shuddering.

By this time the girl reached her car and jumped into the driver's side. It was a rather bright green VW Beetle. The original style, not the newer kind.

Seeing the girl was safe, I returned my attention to the witch. She was walking around in a circle, making odd signs in the air with her hands, sniffing the whole time. Just as she turned in my direction, the car squealed out of the parking area and—

—I was suddenly back in my room holding the journal. I fell back against my pillows, heart racing.

If that wasn't an epic wtf moment, I don't know what is!

Chapter 13

Annie chose that moment to call up the stairs. "Hey Rox, I'm finished. I'm just getting ready to head out. You okay?"

Sitting up, I pulled the silver ring off my finger and shoved it, along with the journals, under my pillows, before quickly heading downstairs to say goodbye to my friend.

"Are you okay?" Annie asked. "You're really pale. You look like you saw a ghost!"

If she only knew.

"Yeah, yeah. I'm fine, honestly. I just realized I haven't eaten breakfast, you know?" I threw out the first excuse I thought of.

"All right, if you're sure. I'll stay a while longer if you need me to. I can make you something to eat," she offered.

"No. No, I'm good. I'm just going to make myself a smoothie or maybe a protein shake today." I thought I did pretty well at keeping the quiver out of my voice, but she still gave me a skeptical look.

"You call me if you need anything, Roxie. I mean it. I've been through this. I know it can just hit you out of the blue sometimes." She paused for a second, waiting to see if I would break down, I think. I just gave her a small nod and what was probably a weak smile, but apparently it was enough.

"Okay. I'll head out, then. If I don't see you or talk to you before the big weekend, take care of yourself. And if you need to talk about crap, or even just talk crap, you call me!" She gave me her sternest mom look and hugged me before leaving.

After she pulled out of drive, I fell back against the wall, palm to my forehead. What big weekend? Ah, the one that Sam had arranged for the four of us to go back to my house and clear my things out. Looking toward the fridge, I decided to skip breakfast. My stomach was still in knots and I was pretty sure nothing I ate would stay down.

Taking a deep breath, I went back up to my room again. The cardio I was getting with these trips up and down the stairs had to be doing some good, I thought distractedly. Buns of steel had to be in my future somewhere. I giggled a little hysterically. Oh god. I was losing it.

I pulled the ring and the journals out from under my pillows. I started to set the ring on top of the nightstand but thought better of it and returned it to the wooden box before taking the journals over to the loveseat in the little reading nook.

Opening the one that had taken me on the weird Alice in Wonderland meets Wizard of Oz trip, I found the spot I had been preparing to read. I looked at the date of the entry. *May, 1961.* I continued reading. *Went out today to see if the rumors were true about a witch sighting in Whigville Cemetery. I know we're not supposed to go out alone, but that site hasn't had any incidents recently that we are aware of. I spotted the witch not long after I arrived, so I made sure to stay downwind of her and out of sight, like we were taught. I thought I could remain hidden long enough to see what she was there for. The wind must have shifted because she looked right at the tree I was hiding behind. I was sure I was a goner. I was too far from the car to make it before she would have caught me but something else seemed to distract her. I looked back but I don't know what she was doing. Once a witch gets your scent, it's pretty much over—isn't that what the Elders always tell us? I made it to the car, only looking back once more before getting out of there. When I told the family about what happened, they sent two of the men out to check but they couldn't find any signs of what had happened, other than the tire marks left on the pavement. I've been forbidden from going out on my own until Grandmam thinks I've learned my lesson. I'm not even allowed to drive my car! R. Blevins.*

That was the end of the entry. Dropping the book into my lap, I looked up, not really focusing on anything in the room. *Had I done that? Had I helped her somehow?* I looked at the entry date again—1961. I wondered how many times a person's mind could be blown before their brain simply exploded.

Looking over at the nightstand, I thought about Rosemary. Maybe she could help me with whatever was going on here. It had been a couple days now so she shouldn't be *too* upset if I called her, right? She hadn't even been as gruff that last time.

I grabbed the jewelry box before I chickened out. The Rose Quartz ring stood out enough from the rest that I didn't even have to root around in there for it. Slipping it on, I closed my eyes and thought of Rosemary, hoping she would be the one to answer instead of Grandma Jenkins. Frowning, I wondered what I would do if Grandma, no *Grandmam,* Jenkins were the one to answer. Shaking my head to clear it, I focused on Rosemary again. Positive thinking, right?

"What is this?"

My eyes flew open. Rosemary was standing there but she wasn't the one that had asked the question. Seeing her with her mouth hanging open, staring at an older woman with the scowl on her face, almost made me laugh. What was it she had said to me? Something about letting flies in? The ferocity in the older woman's face quickly drove those thoughts away.

"Well? Is somebody going to answer me or not?" the older woman looked from Rosemary to me. When she took in the streak in my hair her scowl deepened even more if that was possible. Maybe I should make a hair appointment soon.

Rosemary snapped her mouth shut and looked at me, her expression a little lost.

"Um, hi there?" Well, that was smooth. Trying again, "I'm Roxie, er, Roxanne. I needed to speak to Rosemary so I, um . . ."

"Is she always like this?" the woman asked, turning to Rosemary. "Is this one of Elmer's get?"

Rosemary was still at a loss for words, apparently, because she only shook her head. She looked kind of like she was in shock.

"Well, someone here needs to speak up, quick like. I'm missing my Bingo game!"

That did it. I started laughing. I couldn't help it. Between my experience earlier today and these two now, the thought of this battle ax of an old lady sitting in a Bingo Hall in—wherever it was they now resided—was just too much. Within moments, I was doubled over in the loveseat. If this continued much longer, I was going to have to excuse myself to run for the bathroom before I embarrassed myself. With that thought, my bladder reminded me it was already nearly too late. I jumped up and dashed for the bathroom, practically slamming the door in my haste.

Once business was taken care of and I had composed myself, I studied my reflection in the mirror as I washed my hands. I think I had a new chin hair growing that would need to be plucked out soon. I hated those things, especially the stubby ones. I was stalling before going back out there, I knew. Splashing cold water on my face, I took a few deep breaths and went back into the bedroom.

Both Rosemary and the woman I assumed was Grandmam Jenkins watched me with concern as I walked over and stood next to the bed.

"I'm okay. Just a case of forty-year-old bladder is all." I reassured them. "You must be the infamous Grandmam Jenkins I've heard so much about. I'm pleased to finally meet you." I stuck my hand out toward her. She just looked down at my outthrust hand and then back up at me. The concern on her face gave way to puzzlement.

Ignoring my hand, she turned to Rosemary. "Girl, what is going on here. I need someone to start talking sense."

Rosemary found her voice finally. "I'm not exactly sure, Grandmam. Elmer and I have been working with Roxanne to teach her how some of the jewelry works. It's a bit of a long story."

"How long? Start from the beginning and make it quick. Like I said, I've got things to do."

I let my hand drop. "Rosemary, it's okay. I'll explain. When I'm done, I'll go over why I called for you."

I gave Grandmam the most condensed version I could of what had happened from the time Steven hit me right up until today. Her expression became more incredulous, her brows climbing a little higher the longer I talked. And I had only given her the basic stuff so far.

"What happened to your hair? How long has it been like that?"

My hand flew up to my hair self-consciously. "I think that was from my head injury. Trauma or something maybe."

She nodded, thinking. She looked over at Rosemary and then back at me.

"So, where is Elmer?" she asked slowly.

"He hasn't been doing so well since Rosemary's first, er, appearance. I think he's depressed. Do you want me to call him? He usually answers."

"No. Not yet. I think just us women need to talk for a bit, first."

She eyed me more appraisingly now, looking me over pretty much from head to toe. I fidgeted, as usual, crossing my arms and tucking one under while plucking at my sleeve with the other. Her gaze stopped at the Rose Quartz ring on my right hand. Rosemary stood silently by her side, watching the two of us.

"I've never heard of anyone being able to call someone outside of family back. And never two at a time. You're sure you aren't family, huh?"

"Uh, pretty sure. My parents were part Italian. The other parts are pretty mixed, on both sides. But, there's that whole six degrees thing, you know."

Grandmam, looked over at Rosemary, who just shook her head and shrugged.

"Oh, that's just a saying these days. That we're all only separated by six or fewer connections, that—never mind. I guess it's not important here," I sighed. "I'm not exactly sure how I called you, ma'am. I was thinking of Rosemary, but I had been warned that someone else in the family could show up sometimes, too. I'm still trying to wrap my head around all of this. Sorry I pulled you away from your, um, Bingo, and all, but I just had something really odd happen earlier. It freaked me out pretty bad."

"If you're going to wear that ring, you might as well call me Grandmam," she gave a short laugh. "I don't think I've been called anything else by anyone on this side since the first grand was born." She glanced over at the loveseat, then back at me. "You mind?" she asked, nodding at it.

"No, not at all. Please sit." I said hurriedly. "I'm sorry. I should have offered right away after—well, let's not go back to that. I have no clue what proper etiquette is for all of this. Rosemary, do you want the bed, or I can bring over a chair?"

Rosemary, looked around the room, taking in the chairs on the other side, then went to lean against the wall. "I'm good, thanks. You can take the bed if you want. So, what happened?"

Straight to the point, she was. I sat down on the edge of the bed and continued.

"Well, I decided to study some of the journals, like we discussed. I was wearing the decoder ring," I paused as Rosemary barked a laugh at that, earning her a 'look' from her grandmother. "It's just easier for me if I have something to call each piece. Weird, I know.

"Anyway," I continued. "The journal I was reading was one of the more recent ones, I believe." I looked around for it and spotted it on the little table next to Grandmam. "It was that one. Would you mind?" I gestured to it. She picked the book up, looking at the cover before handing it to me. "Yes, this is the one. I kind of flipped through it for a minute and then one of the entries caught my eye. When I started reading it, well, I got sucked into it."

Rosemary and her grandmother shared a baffled look. "What do you mean you got sucked into it?" Rosemary asked.

"I mean that I was in there. Before I had a chance to read the first word, I got pulled into the story or whatever, and I was there. It was about a girl and a witch in a local cemetery."

Rosemary's eyes widened at this. "Show me which entry."

I turned to the correct page in the little book. "Here, this one." I stood and showed it to her, before returning to the bed.

She skimmed it, looking back at her grandmother, then at me again. "What happened? Tell me all of it, start to finish. From where you were sitting, what you were wearing, everything."

"I, um, I was here on the bed, sitting up against the pillows." I thought back. "I was wearing everything I am now, except for this, of course," I held up my right hand. "I had the other ring on, for the journals. Then, like I said, I was here one second and in the story the next."

I recounted what had happened and what I had seen, right down to the girl squealing the tires of her green VW Beetle during her escape.

Rosemary walked over and sat down heavily on the end of the bed. "How can this be, Grandmam?"

The older woman had been completely silent during the narrative. She didn't answer right away, taking the time again to look me over again, pausing on my gray streak once more. I began fidgeting again, spinning the Rose Quartz ring around my finger nervously.

"What's that?" she asked, pointing to my hands.

I held up my right hand. "Just the ring I used to call you with."

"No. Your other hand."

I started to frown but caught myself. I already had a weird gray streak and other gray hairs creeping in, no need to add wrinkles and more crow's feet. I held up my left hand slowly, palm down. The Ring of Power sparkled like the Hope Diamond on my ring finger. How had I not noticed I was still wearing it from this morning?

"Oh. This. Well, I think that might be another story in itself." I said hesitantly.

"Sounds like a story we need to hear." Grandmam settled herself more deeply into the loveseat and looked at me expectantly.

Chapter 14

Taking a deep breath, I told them about the safe at my house, my missing jewelry, and the cleansing and recharging ritual. Before telling them about what happened when I put the ring into the jewelry box, I reached over and took the box and it's book out of their drawer. I opened the book to the last illustration and handed it to her. "And then there's this."

She paused for a moment before accepting the book. She looked it over before setting it down in her lap.

"Oh, I'm sorry! Here's the ring so you can read it properly," I exclaimed, grabbing the decoder ring out of the box.

She laughed. "I don't need it, dear. Only the living still need something like that to See what Is. Besides, I had this book memorized by the time I was fifteen years old. Unlike some." She slanted a look at Rosemary, who just ignored her.

"I'm sorry, ma'am. I mean Grandmam," I hurriedly corrected myself when she raised her brow at my blunder. I wondered at her phrasing and the emphasis she put on the words. "So, what does this mean? I put my ring in there yesterday, only because I didn't want to lose it. And then there it was, in the book. When I put it on after the cleansing, I just forgot about it." I still felt foolish about that. I mean, the ring was huge, after all. I rarely even wore jewelry so it shouldn't have felt so—natural. Like it belonged on my hand.

"Well, the first thing it means, is that you likely saved Rosemary's life by distracting that witch. We always wondered how it was she escaped unscathed. *How* you did that, I have no idea. If I had to guess, I would say that your ring can affect another Item of Power, which is what everything else in that box is. Since this is pretty much unknown territory, you are going to have to be careful as you learn exactly what it can do. This book," she held up the small illustrated one, "acts like an inventory of sorts, for everything in that box. The magick of the box protects the jewelry in several ways. The book needs to be kept close to it at all times, as the two have a strong link. Since both the box and the book were Crafted for our family, I don't know how or why this happened," she said, holding up the book to indicate my ring's page. "That might just be part of your ring's magic. I've heard of adaptive and complementary types of magick before and that could be what's happening here."

She paused, thinking. "If I were you, I would make sure you get back every last piece of that jewelry your husband took. There are probably pieces that go with the ring that shouldn't be in hands they don't belong in."

I nodded. "I'm working on it. How is it that all of this," I motioned toward the box and the journals, "works for me if I'm not a part of your family?"

"You said Elmer showed you where it was and entrusted it to you? I would say that you are now the official Caretaker. Until you pass this off to someone either in your family or ours, it's your responsibility. That may be part of what's been holding

Elmer here, away from his wife. He wouldn't even realize it, since he was never taught any of this."

"There isn't anybody for me to pass it on to. I don't have any children and I was an only child. I don't even have any cousins that I know of." I panicked a bit at the idea of being stuck here instead of being able to move on when the time came. Then a thought occurred to me. "Wait. I'm not family, and Elmer was able to give me all of this. So that means I can give it to someone else, either now or later, right?"

She shook her head. "There are loopholes, sure. But that's not exactly how it works, Roxanne. Elmer was likely stuck here because there was nobody else close by that could use the Items the way they are meant to be. Until you. Since you have the Sight—and possibly other magicks, if I'm guessing right—he was probably drawn to you as soon as you moved here. Which worked out pretty well for you, from what you told us. These Items, as well as whatever Items were left to you by your family, will be your responsibility to protect and to use. Keep in mind, they will protect you as well. When you are no longer able to perform those duties, your final task will be to find another who can."

"Protect me? Did they protect you? You still died, right?" I was scrambling to process everything she had just said. "They didn't protect Rosemary from that witch. How will they protect me from everything—Other—that's out there?"

"Roxanne. I died of old age, in my sleep. I went peacefully, knowing it was my time. I had already passed everything to Rosemary by then. My job was done," Grandmam chided gently.

Rosemary who had been uncharacteristically silent throughout most of this, added, "I wasn't wearing any of the Items when I went out looking for the witch. I honestly didn't even believe there was a witch out there—none had been seen for years in this area. I was young and stupid." She shook her head in disbelief. "I still can't believe you were the one that saved me."

I snorted as I turned to her. "Really? Your family has had this Sight for who knows how many generations and you've seen everything that you've seen during your life and after. Now I have the Sight, too, all because of a concussion—and possibly brain damage—don't even get me started there, because I'm still expecting to wake up some day and find out this is all some weird coma-induced dream." I had to pause to catch my breath. And for a little dramatic effect, of course. "And *that's* the part you can't believe?"

She laughed at me. "Yes, that's the part, Roxanne. And for the record, I died of a heart attack when I was in my sixties." She patted her thick waistline. "I had high cholesterol and I still chose to eat like I was twenty, so I have nobody to blame but myself. My husband had already passed, and my only child had died in an automobile accident way before her time. I was ready to go be with them. I only stuck around after long enough to make sure Elmer knew where the Items and the journals were."

"So, you've got loved ones on the other side and here I am pulling you back every time I panic or have a question? Oh my gosh—I'm sorry! And why do you not look like you're in your sixties?" Oops. I didn't mean to add that last part out loud. She really didn't look much older than fifty.

"It's not like that. This is part of our job description. One day it will be part of yours, too. Coming back to this side is kind of nice, once in a while. Change of scenery and all that, you know. And thanks, it's these extra pounds that help keep the wrinkles at bay," she said with a saucy wink.

"If you girls are done over there, can we get back to the matter we're here for in the first place? I would like to get back to my Bingo game before all the good prizes are gone."

What kind of prizes did they give away in Hea—er, the other side, I wondered. Deciding it wasn't a good time to ask that question, I moved on to something else I had been wondering.

"Elmer mentioned that I must have had at least a little Sight when I was younger. That maybe I grew out of it and the head injury just turned it back on, like a switch. Does that sound feasible to you?"

Grandmam Jenkins thought about that before answering. "I suppose it's possible something like that could happen." She gave a pointed look at the ring on my left hand. "After everything I've heard today, there's not much that I would doubt. He is right about you having the Sight—or something like it, anyway—at some point in your life. Especially if your family has its own Items. Abilities don't just show up out of the blue. Family lineage is what determines these things. And different families' magicks can evolve and change sometimes, just like everything else. It's just the nature of things. You do look much like others with the Sight that I've met before—outside my own family, of course—," she squinted at me, "but there are some differences."

"Like what?" I asked, not sure if I was curious or worried.

"You're brighter around the edges, for one thing," she said.

Rosemary nodded her agreement and piped in, "And your color is a little different. Our family's edges are more white. Yours looks kind of silverish."

"Uh-huh. Are you sure you aren't just picking up the gray hairs poking through? Because I'm pretty sure my gray has doubled in the past month."

Both Rosemary and her grandmother guffawed at that. Great. At least I was a source of amusement to them.

"So, what now? I know you ladies have to get back to, um, Bingo and everything, but what should I do now?"

"*Now* you study. You read the journals, you learn what each of those Items do, and you get that jewelry back from your husband so you can learn about those, too. You'll need to start keeping your own journal. It's how we keep records. Did your family have journals that they left you?"

I didn't correct her about my husband, just as I hadn't at her last mention of him. In my mind, he was my soon-to-be-ex-husband. "I never saw any when I cleared their things out of the house. I do have some boxes of photo albums and papers that I've never gone through, except to pull pictures for their funerals. It's all still boxed up over at the house." I glanced over at my laptop. "I can keep a journal. I write a lot anyway, so I've always got notebooks handy, but—could I keep record on my computer, too?"

Grandmam looked at Rosemary, confused. Rosemary explained, "These days people use computers to document most things. It's like a typewriter but it stores what you type inside."

I didn't correct her explanation. There was no way I was going to try to explain what cloud storage was to these two. Or a memory card or any other backup device.

"I guess you could do that if you wanted to," she responded, though her tone clearly conveyed she really couldn't understand why anyone *would* want to. "You'll figure it all out, I'm sure. You need to talk to Elmer and let him know it's time for him to cross over. He has loved ones that have waited a long time to be with him again."

She stood up and Rosemary followed suit. I guess that was the signal that the visit was over. Grandmam handed me back the book with the illustrations in it as I got up, as well.

"You keep these safe, girl. And yourself, too. If you need either of us, you pull us over right away, you hear?" The way she said it was more of an order than a question, but I nodded anyway.

"I will, ma'am." I promised, then corrected myself quickly before she could. "I mean Grandmam."

My answer seemed to satisfy her because she relaxed and looked over at Rosemary, who was poking through the jewelry box. "Let's go. Does she know what to do?"

"Yes, Grandmam." Rosemary sounded exasperated. "I've only been here twice but I have not been completely remiss, you know." As she walked over to stand next to Grandmam, she bumped my hand. Reflexively, I looked down and opened my hand as she dropped a ring into it. It was the ring she had told me to wear whenever I went out, that would afford at least a little protection against Steven. She looked back at me and mouthed 'wear it', and then looked pointedly at the ring on my left hand. I slipped the ring on and gave her a small nod.

"Humph! You should have told me about all of this yourself."

"All of what? I only knew she had the Items and the books—"

"And you didn't think any of that was important?"

Good grief. It was definitely time to send these two back to the other side. Before I even finished the thought, they were gone. I blinked at the sudden silence. I hadn't even wished Grandmam good luck at Bingo.

Flopping back on the bed, I waited for my brain to explode.

Chapter 15

Elmer seemed even more withdrawn the next morning. I needed to tell him about my meeting with his cousin and grandmother, but I wasn't quite sure how to bring it up with his current mood. I mentioned going to the dog park, thinking we could talk on the way there and maybe I could just work it into our conversation. He declined, insisting he wasn't up to it, that he felt too distracted.

Maybe I'll just take Jake and I can work this through in my head. I'll talk to him when we get back.

"Hey Jake. Want to go to the park with me?" I asked, watching Elmer out of the corner of my eye. He didn't look up at us or even respond to Jake's happy bark.

"Okay then, I'll take that as a yes. Elmer, we'll be back in a bit. Will you be around later?"

He nodded, still not looking at either of us.

It *was* a beautiful day for a walk, it turned out. I fingered the opal pendant I had decided to wear, though I didn't really expect to run into anything Other at the park. The weight of it felt odd but I guess that was a small price to pay for some measure of safety.

As soon as we entered the drive to the rear parking lot of the McFarlen Library, where the head of the walking trail and the entrance to the dog park were located, I noticed a woman getting out of a white commercial-looking Sprinter van. She had a beautiful German Shepherd at her side. The dog was panting excitedly and gave a couple little hops but was careful not to pull on the leash. His owner was busy talking on her cell phone, not paying the slightest attention to him as she grabbed a few things out of her van.

I skirted around her, giving the dog a wide berth in case he was protective, but he had focused on something behind me. I glanced back, seeing Jake stopped in his tracks, looking back at the other dog.

Huh. It's almost like they can see each other. Is that possible?

"Come on, boy," I said, clapping my hand lightly against my thigh. Jake moved up to my side. The German Shepherd dog paused mid-step, head cocked, his eyes following Jake. The woman on the phone wasn't paying attention to her dog and walked right into him, nearly falling.

"Rocco!" she yelled at him, slapping his nose. "Move! What are you trying to do, kill me?"

The poor dog yipped at the slap, his ears drooping back dejectedly as the woman gave his leash a hard pull. He gave a last woeful look back at us as he followed the woman into the park, the cell phone occupying her attention fully once more.

I stood there for a moment, in shock. Should I have said something? Done something? Feeling sorry for poor Rocco, I looked down at Jake. "Maybe this wasn't such a great idea, boy. You still want to do this?"

He woofed and looked over toward the park. I swore sometimes he understood me. "Okay, then. Let's go. How about we sit far away from her, hmm?"

As we walked over to the gate leading into the park, I noticed a man by the fence watching the woman and Rocco. She was sitting on one of the benches, still on her phone. Rocco was sitting beside her, quivering with excitement, wanting to play with the other dogs. As she reached down and unsnapped his collar, I saw the dog lean away from her slightly, his head down a bit. I didn't know much about dogs, but he acted like he didn't want to be hit again. As soon as he was released, he ran off to play with a couple of the other dogs.

"Oh, Jake. Poor Rocco. Someone needs to report her." I said, as I went through the gate, holding it open for him. I shook my head and muttered to myself as the bear of a dog simply ghosted through the fence instead, taking off running and barking happily to play. I watched as he ran over to join two other dogs chasing a ball their human threw. Both dogs avoided Jake's personal space, just as he took special care to stay out of theirs. Curious. I wondered if the dogs could somehow sense him there.

"His real name is Toby," the man at the fence said. He sounded like he was speaking with his teeth clenched together. "And she doesn't deserve him. That imitation Cruella Deville doesn't deserve my dog."

I turned to look back at him, carefully keeping the fence between us. The man looked angry. "Um, excuse me?" I asked, hesitantly, not sure if I should even be engaging him in conversation.

His head snapped toward me so fast, I nearly tripped stepping back. Looking back over at Jake, knowing he wouldn't let this man hurt me, I straightened and stared back at him.

His brow scrunched in confusion. He looked down for a moment and then back at me. "You can see me?"

"Y-Yes, I can see you. What kind of question is that?" I asked, wondering how fast Jake could make it back here if I screamed. I looked down at the ring Rosemary had told me to wear. Would it really protect me?

He looked back at the woman. And then at Rocco—or Toby, as he'd called him. And then back at me.

"Um, so, is this like a divorce thing? She got the dog?" I asked.

He made a sound of disgust. "Not hardly. She wasn't even my type when I was alive."

I stiffened. "Y-you're a ghost?"

The man turned to face me fully. He was kind of handsome, in a dark and dangerous kind of way. The way he held himself, almost at attention, made me think he was military for some reason.

He considered me for a moment then, stepping closer said, "The name's Randall, ma'am. Randall James. My friends call me—used to call me—Rand. I'm sorry for the way I behaved. You startled me, is all. You're the first person who's seen me in—a really long time. I guess I wasn't expecting it. May I ask what your name is?"

"I'm Roxanne, but my friends call me Roxie." I was nervous and desperately hoped it didn't show. He might be kind of a hunk but I was still in shock that he was a ghost. I was trying to figure out how I hadn't noticed that right away. Looking more closely now, I could tell he looked less solid than a—living—person normally would. Maybe it was because I had been with Jake all morning and was getting too used to how he looked. "Do you mind?" I asked, pointing at a nearby bench. "I brought Jake here for some playtime with the other dogs."

He looked around at the other people in the area so intensely, I wondered if he was memorizing every detail. "Of course not. That big black monster, he's yours?"

Nodding, I decided not to tell him Jake wasn't actually mine. After yesterday, I wasn't ready to spill the insanity of my last month to a complete stranger within the first minute. Brushing off the empty bench, I made sure there were no surprises on it before sitting down and answering. I watched Jake getting his exercise, taking my time as I gathered my thoughts.

"So how is it that you're here? A ghost hanging out at a dog park? And how is it that you can see Jake?" I asked him, still watching the dogs.

"That's a bit of a long story, ma'am. And why would you think I wouldn't see him?" he asked.

I thought about it for a moment, chewing on my lip. "I'm not really sure. I'm kind of new to this, you see. I'm still trying to figure out how it all works. I was learning everything I could from Elmer—"

"Elmer? Is he someone like you? A person that can see spirits?" Rand interrupted.

"No, well, yes. I mean, he was when he was alive. He had the Sight, like I do, that is—he was able to See ghosts or, um, spirits? But he called himself a ghost, not a spirit."

Rand looked around the park, searching. "Is he here with you?"

"Oh. No, he decided not to come today. He usually does though. I think he's considering crossing over finally. He really misses his wife."

He processed that for a moment. "You mean going into the light?"

I nodded.

"I see. Good for him! That makes me very happy to hear."

"Why do you say that?" I asked.

He frowned and looked at the ground in thought for a moment before answering, "The light that beckons to us to cross—to say that it's a very strong calling, well, that would be an understatement. Most spirits go immediately—after. But some of us, like me, have matters here that need to be resolved before we do. The fact that your friend has resolved his issue is great. I only hope that I can do the same one day . . ."

I wanted to ask what matter was important enough to keep him here, but that seemed really personal, so I bit my lip. Studying him from under my lashes, I had to admit that he was definitely an attractive man. Heck, who was I kidding? He was drop-dead gorgeous. Pun intended. And *way* out of my league, even as a ghost. For a second I felt guilty for even thinking any of that—I was in the middle of a divorce, after all. But, hey, divorced isn't dead, right? And, if I was honest with myself, I felt really comfortable around him, safe even, now that I was talking to him. I didn't want to say or do anything to make him disappear on me just yet. He was the most normal seeming ghost or spirit I had met so far. Maybe if my life wasn't so insane right now—but if it wasn't, I could be standing right next to him and never even know. I shook my head to dispel that disturbing train of thought.

"Jake is actually Elmer's dog," I confessed. "Elmer stayed because he was afraid Jake couldn't go with him to the same place when he died. He felt guilty leaving him because Jake had stayed with him after *his* death."

"That actually happens a lot more than you'd think with animals and older people," Rand said, nodding.

"He tells me how much he misses his wife Birdie, over and over again. I need to convince him that it's okay to go to be with her, that it's time. And that I can keep Jake company and out of trouble because—well, I can see him, and I kind of owe him. He saved my life," I admitted. "But I'm really torn. What if I need to learn more from him before he goes?"

"What more would you need to know?"

I laughed. "Oh, pretty much everything." Good lord, this almost felt like flirting. I hadn't flirted in over a decade.

"I may be able to help answer *some* of your questions," he offered. "It's kind of mind-boggling actually just how much there is in the paranormal world and the shadow world that I had absolutely no clue existed before I died. And I'm still learning a lot of it myself."

There was my chance. He'd opened the door, after all. "Um, may I ask how you died and what made you stay here afterward?" I immediately felt guilty.

Smooth Roxie! Real Smooth.

He leaned over, almost conspiratorially. "Just so you know, you need to be aware of the fact that you're talking to nobody, as far as the rest of the world is concerned. Just a tip that may save you some embarrassment. That girl that just walked past us noticed. Big time."

I glanced around now, more than embarrassed that I hadn't even considered this problem.

"But sure, I don't mind telling you," he continued, politely ignoring my flaming cheeks. "I was an Army Ranger, home on leave, between deployments. I waded through so much action over in the sandbox that you wouldn't believe it, and came home without a scratch. I walked into a convenience store here one day to buy a beer and ran straight into some punk with a pistol robbing the place. He didn't even know how to hold the weapon properly, but he was lucky enough to get one in my heart. Go figure. He got away with it too. He killed the girl behind the counter, for whatever petty amount of cash she had in the drawer, and walked right back out the front door. No surveillance cameras to be found. I couldn't let that stand, so I passed on my first chance at the light. Later, I found that my dog Toby had been taken out of my truck by animal control and placed in the pound. No way was I letting him get euthanized, so I stayed with him. This chick that adopted him gets zero points for doggie parent of the year, so I've continued to turn down the offer when the light beckons, while looking for a better opportunity for him. And to look for the punk that killed me. I *will* find him, and he *will* pay."

"Oh, that's quite a story! I'm so sorry that all of that happened to you. And thank you for your service, by the way. Were you married? Have kids? Any of that?" The questions just spilled out, right past my filter.

Seriously? Word vomit much?

"Thank you. No, and . . . no! I think."

The thought of what he'd do to the guy when he found him made me shiver a little bit. A Ranger? *They're supposed to be really tough. And strong.* For a second, I felt a flush of warmth. I hoped it was because I was sitting next to an attractive guy, er, ghost, and not just a hot flash.

"So, what about you? Have you always had the Sight? I'm guessing not, since you said you're new at this?"

Fair question, I suppose. And it's been more than a minute now, right?

"I suffered a head injury recently. It started right after that."

"Car accident?"

"I wish. No, more like domestic violence."

"I'm sorry. Are you safe now?"

"Yes, I am. I'm staying with my best friend, unwinding my marriage, and starting over with weird ghost vision. I'm taking it a day at a time, just trying to deal with my new normal, I guess."

I stopped myself before I spilled too much personal information. I really didn't want to scare him off with an emotional outburst. He started to say something, but stopped, looking over my head. He looked concerned, but not with me, I thought.

Jake came bounding over with a threatening woof, placing himself between Rand and me. I moved over quickly to avoid getting frostbite. I laughed to show him things were good. "It's okay boy, this is Rand. He's a friend, but thank you for looking out for me!" And then it hit me, "Hey! You can see him! Rand, Jake can see you!"

"Yes Ma'am, it seems he can," Rand agreed, looking puzzled. With me.

"We're both spirits Ma'am. All spirits can see all other spirits."

"Hey, knock it off with the ma'am stuff. Call me Roxie, or Roxanne if you're feeling formal." He did have a point, though. Jake could see Elmer and vise versa. It made sense that Rand and Jake would be able to see each other, too.

"Okay . . . Roxie!" he laughed. "That is one *big* protector you have there! I want to check something out. Toby! To me," he yelled.

My eyes scanned for Toby, finding him right where he was the last time I'd seen him. He stopped instantly and came running full speed to Rand. Jake protested with a deep woof and a growl. Toby bravely stopped with his body in front of Rand but did nothing to challenge the huge beast in front of him.

"Well, look at that! I think Toby can see Jake too," Rand exclaimed.

"You're right, he can. It's okay, Jake. Hey, Toby, good boy. We're all friends here," I said in a soothing voice.

"Toby can see me, but I didn't know if he could see other spirits," he explained.

Canine posturing now dispensed with; the two dogs began checking each other out. Jake was obviously surprised that Toby could see him, and he seemed overjoyed by the fact. Toby looked confused when he tried to sniff Jake's face and his snout went right through him. Sitting back on his haunches, he sneezed a couple of times, cocking his head in confusion as he wiped at his nose with his paw. Jake chuffed and dropped his front end to the ground, his furry butt in the air, tail wagging wildly. I had never had a dog, but even I knew this was dogspeak for 'let's play'. And play they did—it became immediately apparent that Jake had found a new friend. They raced around playing the oddest game of tag I had ever seen.

"I bet people think Toby's 'not quite right' after watching him jumping around and chasing nothing like that!" Rand laughed.

"You seem to be pretty in tune with the people around us. Is that a military thing? Being careful not to be noticed?" I asked.

"Yes, ma—I mean Roxie. We observe and we never quit training. Not even when it becomes automatic and part of who we are."

"Oh, I'm not complaining. I just noticed, is all. That's kind of what *I* do. Notice things. Pay attention to the details more than most folks."

"That's probably because of your Sight. It would definitely affect who you are, like that."

"Elmer said lots of kids can See when they're young, but most grow out of it believing what their parents told them about it just

145

being an overactive imagination. He thinks I was one of those." I laughed ruefully. "My mother always said I used to see scary things where nobody else did when I was really little. I hardly remember it now, it's like it's at the very edge of my memory. When it went away or maybe I outgrew it, nobody gave it another thought."

Toby's new owner must have taken her nose out of her phone and looked for him because she called him, and was giving us the stink eye. "Let's go Toby," Rand said, turning that way.

It was hard to admit, but it bothered me for a minute when he ran off. Just for a minute. But when he turned and yelled, "Hope to see you tomorrow Roxie!"? I did have to admit, I felt relieved. Maybe even a little more than relieved.

Are you kidding me? I'm not even divorced yet. And *he's a ghost or spirit or—whatever!*

Chapter 16

"Elmer! You'll never guess what happened today!" I called out as soon as I was sure Sam wasn't home yet. For once, he appeared right where I was looking without scaring the crap out of me.

"Roxanne, you seem rather excited. Is everything alright?"

"Yes, well, at least I think so."

The whole story came spilling out about how I'd met Rand and Toby. By the time I was done telling Elmer everything, his expression had completely changed. He seemed excited that Toby could not only see Jake, but play with him too.

"That's wonderful, Roxanne! I assume these new friends must live around here somewhere? Do you think you'll see them there again?"

"I'm not exactly sure but I would think so—the last thing Rand said to me was that he hoped to see me there again tomorrow."

"Well then, dear girl, I suppose we'd all better be prepared to make a day of it there tomorrow then, shall we?"

"I think that sounds like a plan," I agreed. Elmer looked pleased. Almost like a picture-perfect grandfather type of pleased. I was relieved to see him almost back to his original self. Well, his ghost self, anyway.

Jake woofed softly to get our attention, and then disappeared. That didn't even seem odd to me now.

"Looks like all that playing has made my old friend tired," Elmer said. "He's probably out for the night now. Thank you for making my Jake so very happy, Roxanne." He almost teared up at that. "I think I'll go cuddle up with him and rest. It appears that you may have fulfilled one of my promises for me." With that, he was gone too.

"Wait. What?" Did that mean he was ready to cross over? Huh. Maybe convincing him it was time wouldn't be as difficult as I thought.

***

The next day almost felt like a 'meet-the-parents' day with a new boyfriend kind of thing to me. Talk about strange. I ended up spending quite a bit of extra time in front of the mirror, and had changed my clothes three times before heading downstairs. The last thing I wanted was to be too obvious with the way I looked, but I wanted to look good at the same time. It had been a long time since I'd felt these feelings and I wasn't sure how I even felt about any of it, yet.

"Well, don't you look pretty today," Elmer told me from the bar stool at which he sat when I arrived in the kitchen. Jake stood by the sliding glass door, looking eagerly outside. Not laying— standing! "Is that a new ring?" he asked, noticing the ring on my left hand. "I think I recognize the one on your other hand from the box. You must be getting more comfortable with everything, I take it?"

"Yes, kind of. I'll tell you all about it when we get back. And you are certainly looking pretty spiffy yourself there, Elmer. Looking to make a good impression today, are you?" I smiled, tucking both hands behind my back. It felt weird still, wearing these rings, but I wasn't going to turn down any extra help I could get.

"Of course!"

I wanted to ask Elmer what he'd meant about me fulfilling one of his promises last night, but something told me to just wait for now. I needed to talk to him about everything else that had happened since I found this ring. I took a deep breath, letting it out slowly. It would all work out, right? *It's not all about you Roxie, the promise he mentioned probably has something to do with Jake. Elmer has a lot of love for him.*

"Ready?" I asked. Things *would* work out, I repeated to myself.

***

Jake didn't even wait for me to open the gate into the park. He saw Toby playing with some others and with a mighty woof, ran right through it—ghost style. As I opened it for Elmer and myself, I noticed the beaming smile on his face. His eyes were locked on Jake, who was greeting his new friend Toby. The German Shepherd immediately stopped what he'd been doing at the sight of his gigantic friend.

"Can you tell they like one another?" I chuckled.

"That makes me *so* happy to see," Elmer answered.

We headed toward my favorite out-of-the-way bench, where Rand already sat waving. As we walked up to him he stood and introduced himself. "Hello sir. My name is Randall James. Rand for short, sir."

"Hello Rand. Elmer Jenkins. Pleased to meet you." His eyes went to where the dogs ran some imaginary obstacle course. "Seems our pups have become fast friends, eh?"

"Yes, sir! Toby can't get enough of your big ole boy Jake. That's the biggest dog I've ever laid eyes on. What does—did—he weigh in at?"

"Over a buck fifty last time he was at the vet. Are you ex-military? Don't hear too much of the 'sir' stuff these days."

"Army, sir. Ranger."

"Well, that's enough 'sirs', okay?" Elmer said, smiling.

Rand just smiled back at him. "Good morning, Roxanne," he greeted me.

Raising a brow, I looked at him questioningly. *Why is he using my formal name in front of Elmer?*

I heard someone holler, "Hey! What about your dog?" and looked up. Toby's—or Rocco's as she called him—human was outside the gate walking towards her van.

"Oh, he'll be alright. I'm just going to a restaurant for breakfast. I can't very well take him there, can I? I'll be right back."

Elmer looked angry. It was the first time I'd seen that expression on him. Rand mumbled something I'm sure I didn't want to hear under his breath, and the person hollering at her was just shaking her head. I had never owned a dog before, but even I knew that was a dangerous situation to put Toby in. Thank goodness we were here.

"She does that all the time," Rand told Elmer. "Cruella lives out of her van, and thinks this park is her own personal doggie day-care center for my Toby. She doesn't deserve him."

Elmer looked slightly confused, so Rand told him the story of how she'd wound up with Toby. I took out a ball I'd picked up along the path on the way here, called Toby, and threw it. The person who'd been hollering smiled and waved at me, seeing I was looking out for him. I gave her a wave back as both Toby and Jake took off like a shot after the ball, wrestling over it—as best they could since they couldn't actually touch one another—until finally Toby brought it back for me to throw again.

While I threw the ball for the dogs, Elmer and Rand traded stories about them. Toby had at one time been in training to be a cadaver dog for the Michigan State Police. He'd been passed over for being too easily distracted, according to his official record.

"I know now that what they thought was him being an air-head, was really his Sight," Rand told Elmer. "He was Seeing and reacting to the spirit of the dead body, which in many cases had not yet crossed over. When my buddy there told me that Toby would be available for adoption, I jumped at the chance. He was without a doubt, the smartest dog I'd ever met, and I had pretty much come to the decision that I was pushing my luck by accepting any more deployments. I was ninety-nine percent that I was going to position myself for a State-side assignment from now on, and he would be the perfect companion dog for me. He was, too, until that punk at the convenience store got lucky." He proceeded to tell Elmer the whole story of what happened to him.

Elmer said he totally understood why Rand had passed over his chances at the light so far while looking for a better opportunity for Toby. He also counseled him that spending too much effort on getting even with the thug who'd killed him was not only a waste, but it was bad karma to boot.

"I have been torn daily, for years, between crossing through to be with my Birdie when the light beckons and staying here with Jake so he wasn't lonely, afraid, or miserable. I guess you could say I've been looking for a better opportunity for him, as well. I don't have control of my house since I died. My children sold it to a single woman who has no idea we're even there. Otherwise, I'd take Toby home in a heartbeat if I had someone to care for him."

"Yeah, it's too bad. Those boys really seem to get along," Rand agreed. "I guess an arrangement like that would just about take care of my worries for him and take away my excuse for not crossing over, but the longer I'm here as a spirit, the less sure I am that I want to. Have you ever thought about that Elmer?"

Rand wasn't talking to me, but I was right here. It wasn't like I was eavesdropping or anything. I almost groaned. I needed to convince Elmer to go, not stay. And Rand? *Does he really want revenge that bad on the person who killed him, or does he maybe have another reason to consider sticking around on this side?* That thought gave me tingles that I hadn't felt in a very long time. *Surely I wasn't an influence on his wanting to stay here?*

I blew out a small sigh of relief when Elmer responded. "No. I love my children and my grandchildren, but they showed little interest in having an old man around even when I was alive. I think about going to be with my Birdie every day, but I keep telling myself that when I do we'll have forever together, at least as far as I know we will. I can't let myself risk Jake's existence here becoming an unhappy one, just because of my being in a hurry." He snuck a look in my direction, thinking I hadn't noticed. "I take my responsibility to him very seriously, but I think right now, he's happier than he's been in his whole life. If I thought things would stay this way for him, I think I could allow myself to go over."

Now Rand snuck a peek my way. "Roxie has as much told me that she owes her life to you two, and that she's already offered to keep him company and look after him in your place. You should take her up on it!" He caught me when my head snapped back his way, but he didn't let on to Elmer.

"Something's about to change," Elmer told him. "I can sense it. Now if I could just figure out a way to have it both ways, I think I'd go."

"What? What do you mean by that?" Rand asked.

"I haven't got it all figured out yet, my boy, but I'll get there," Elmer told him.

Both dogs came racing up to the three of us, exhausted from all the running they'd been doing. That signaled the end of the guys talking "in private." I had a pretty good idea of what Elmer was thinking now. If he knew there was a way that I could call him back from the other side periodically to see Jake and check on him . . . and then Elmer locked eyes with me, and he smiled! He'd known that I was listening in, the entire time.

What a sly fox!

About two hours after she'd left, Cruella came back. She had her arms full as she struggled to get through the gate. A folding lawn chair, a book bag, a McDonald's bag, a Starbucks coffee, and, of course, her ever-present phone. We watched her openly, along with everyone else in the park as she set up camp under the closest tree to the gate. "Rocco!" she called. "Rocco! Come here!" she repeated, aggravated. Seeing Toby at my side once again, she gave me a suspicious look.

Toby whined his displeasure, but dutifully trotted over to her. She reached into the McDonald's bag, unwrapped a hamburger, and tossed it at his feet. Then, without a word, or giving him anything to drink, she opened her book. Toby wolfed it down and whined again as he licked up errant crumbs off the ground. He was obviously hungry. Then, as he'd probably done before, he trotted over to another person with a water dish and water bottle they'd brought along, drinking deeply before running back to where Jake waited.

"She has no business having a dog," Rand said absently under his breath.

"No. She certainly does not," Elmer agreed.

"I know one thing for sure," I said to them both, "I'll be packing some proper dog food, water, and a dish for Toby from now on when I come. I'll feed him when she leaves him here alone. Eating hamburgers just can't be healthy for a beautiful dog like him."

"Thank you," Rand said. "You don't know how much I would appreciate your doing that."

I could tell by the look in his eyes that he meant every word. I hadn't said it for attention. I considered it basic decency and respect for any creature, especially one as great as Toby. It was clear that Cruella Deville, as we called her, was the wrong human for him.

We need to figure out a way to help Toby.

Chapter 17

I was surprised to see Elmer sitting at the snack bar when I came downstairs the next morning. "Good morning!" I greeted him. At the sound of my voice, Jake appeared beside him.

"Good morning Roxanne. I've been waiting for you. I'm afraid that my mind hasn't given me a moment's rest since my revelation at the park yesterday while talking with Rand. And, before you say anything—yes, I knew you could hear me. I just didn't want to give anything away to Rand, just yet. That's your decision to make, but I'd like to talk to you about my idea."

He paused, before continuing slowly, "Roxanne, what if I *could* have it both ways? What if I crossed over, but could be called back to visit with Jake from time to time? Ever since Rosemary told me what she did about Birdie missing me so, and wondering *why* I haven't joined her, it's really been haunting me. I don't want her thinking that I no longer love her or anything, you know?"

This was exactly the opening I had been waiting for. To say I had mixed feelings was an understatement, but I knew this was the right thing to do. Time to suck it up and just rip the band-aid off.

"About that Elmer. We need to talk." I said, taking a seat next to him.

"Okay. Is everything alright?" he asked, instantly concerned.

"It's fine. Or it's going to be anyway. Just hear me out until the end. This is going to take me a little while to tell you everything." And it did. I started at the point where I found my ring and ended at Rosemary and his grandmother leaving two days ago. I tried to make sure I left nothing out, especially the fact that I was able to bring both women over at once. Oh, and that his job here was done and he would feel the pull to cross even more strongly. It hadn't occurred to me then but, as I was telling him about it now, I realized there hadn't been any energy drain to me that day. At all. Looking down at the ring, I suspected it had something to do with that.

When I was done, there was silence. Elmer slumped back in his chair, staring at the space in front of him, just processing it all. I waited, trying not to fidget, then decided I really needed coffee for the rest of the conversation I knew was coming.

"I don't know what to say, Roxanne," he said finally.

I huffed out a breath as I sat down again, closing my eyes for a second as I took my first sip of coffee before looking back at him. "About which part?"

He looked over at me with both eyebrows raised. "Any of it. I've never heard of any of what you did that day being done before. Granted, none of the men ever got the training that our women did with the Items, but we still knew about them. We heard the stories, read the journals, and so forth. Sometimes we'd even see a bit of it firsthand, but—nothing like this."

That reminded me. "I have a question about that, Elmer. About the men and the women thing. If it's only the women who used the Items, recorded everything, trained or passed down the knowledge—what exactly did the men do?"

He cackled at that. "Well, besides the obvious? We were the muscle in many cases. We'd watch over the women, when needed. We were the primary breadwinners, just like in normal, non-Seeing families."

"Not to be dense here, but what do you mean by 'the obvious'?" I wondered.

"Aren't you a little old for me to be telling you about the birds and the bees, Roxanne? We helped to keep the bloodlines going," he said, with a mischievous glint in his eye.

"Okay, mister, first off, you never call any woman old unless you are trying to insult her and you're at a safe enough distance to dodge things being thrown at you. Or you want to eat shoe leather for dinner for a week or three." I ignored the idea of old people sex. Even though technically I was old people, too.

He chuckled. "I think I'm safe on both those counts. But, this? Roxanne, this is—amazing!" He shook his head in awe. "How was Grandmam? Did she say anything about Birdie?"

The hope in his eyes was nearly too much for me. "Just that she's waiting for you, Elmer. That it's time for you to seriously start thinking about crossing over to be with her."

"But there's Jake, I have to think about him. And what about Toby? Something needs to be done about that woman. That dog needs a real home, with someone who will take proper care of him. Do you think—" he paused. I could almost see his thoughts racing. "Do you think you could bring Toby here? Would Sam be okay with that? If you could convince that woman to do the right thing and think about what's best for him?"

"Let me worry about Toby. I'll work it all out, Elmer. Somehow. Jake is comfortable enough with me that he'll be just fine. I promise you don't have to worry about either of them. It's time to think about yourself now."

If I could somehow convince Cruella to give Toby up, would Sam be okay with the big German Shepherd staying here? Years ago she talked about getting a dog but eventually decided her schedule kept her away too much. Come to think of it, I realized that I hadn't even seen her much in the last two days. She was gone before I came down and had some big case or something she was working on that was keeping her at the office later than usual. The brief moments I did see her, she seemed somewhat distracted.

Elmer's next comment snapped me back to the present. His voice was shaking with excitement. "I can't believe I can finally go to be with her. When do you think I should go? I want to talk to that Rand fellow again first, for sure."

"Rand? Why? What's he got to do with any of this?" I could feel the heat in my cheeks rising, so I ducked my head and took another drink of my coffee.

Elmer wasn't fooled in the least. "Someone needs to watch over you. You're still new enough to all of this that having someone like him around could make a difference for you." He put a hand up to halt my attempted objections. "I know you said Rosemary and Grandmam told you to call on them whenever you need, but what if you're in a position where you can't? This town may not be the biggest draw for Others, but that doesn't mean there aren't any. Plus, if you have Toby, he's going to want to be around anyway. I'm thinking he would be a gentleman about certain matters but I'm still going to have a discussion with him. Just because I'm a ghost, doesn't mean I can't give a young buck like him what for."

I didn't even know what to say to that. On the one hand, I was deeply touched. Barely remembering either of my grandfathers, Elmer was the closest thing I would probably ever have to that experience. But, on the other hand? "Elmer, seriously? I'm forty years old, almost forty-one! And I'm not even his type, I'm sure, even with the whole still-having-a-heartbeat thing notwithstanding." Those objections sounded weak, even to me. "And Toby, well, if he's taken care of, Rand may just choose to cross, too."

At that, I stopped to wonder. Would he feel he could cross over if Toby was taken care of? Even though I had only just met Rand, the thought of him crossing over made my heart hurt a little. I did feel safe when I was near him but I didn't want him to feel obligated to stay on this side because Elmer guilted him into it. And really, how much protection could a ghost actually be?

As if sensing my thoughts, Jake looked up at me and woofed. Well, he did have a point. "Yes, Jake, you're the best. Did I ever thank you, big guy?" He woofed again more softly and lay his head back down.

Elmer looked at me questioningly. I shrugged sheepishly. Jake was probably just excited about hearing Toby's name mentioned several times.

"Be that as it may, I still want to talk to him. I'll cross as soon as I know everything is as it should be." He stopped as another thought occurred to him. "Will you be able to call me back to see Jake every once in a while? I don't want him to forget about me. I'll be able to tell Birdie all about him. She's been wondering, surely."

"I think so, but I'm still learning about how all this works. Do you think there's any reason it *wouldn't* work?"

"I don't really know. You've been able to do things that aren't supposed to be possible. Or at the very least, have never been done before." He laughed ruefully. "Those old hens are probably still clucking about it over there, trying to figure out what's different about you."

"Elmer, didn't we just go over what can happen when you call a woman old? Adding *hen* won't earn you any points with any woman, relative or not." I joked, but his comment worried me. I was different, not to mention I wasn't family. They had already warned me that might mean everything could react unpredictably.

"Grandmam always could find a mean switch," he shot back. Then he went on more soberly, "But I don't know anything about how all that stuff works with the Items, for sure. When I showed signs of having the Sight, my mother took me to spend time learning with her older sister, Mary, and her niece—my cousin, Rosemary. They lived with my Grandmam and Grandpappy." I could tell he was going to head down memory lane for a little stroll, but I let him. I didn't know how much more time I would have with him and I did enjoy listening to his history. "Aunt Mary, she had the Sight, too. Rosemary was the last woman in the family to have the Sight that I know of. She took over after Grandmam and Aunt Mary were gone. She had a daughter, Rosemary did. She was the spitting image of her mama, too. But our little Rosie died too young in a car accident, in her senior year of high school. Rosemary was never the same after that. We had been close before, you know, Rosemary and I. She was right there as a witness when Birdie and I were married." He sighed heavily. "Anyway, even though I was sent to learn, the women were taught a lot more than the men were. We weren't allowed to use the Items—we rarely even handled them. That Rose Quartz ring was only spoken of and, as far as I know, only female ancestors were called on with it."

He seemed to be talked out for the moment. "Elmer, what's the worst that could happen if I did call you? Is there any chance you could get stuck over here? I don't want to do anything that would hurt you." Another thought occurred to me. " You know, I could always send updates back with Rosemary about how Jake is doing. I'm sure she wouldn't mind relaying messages from you, either."

I wanted to reach out and rub his back soothingly, but I knew how that would end up for me, so I wrapped my hands firmly around my still-warm coffee cup.

He gave Jake a long look. "I suppose that will have to do. But, you will at least try, won't you?"

"How about this—I'm going to ask Rosemary about it first and see what she thinks. *If* she thinks it's safe, I'll try." I promised him.

He nodded, looking depressed again. I leaned toward him. "Elmer. Birdie is waiting for you over there. I know you want to see her again. Jake is going to be just fine. Really."

Chapter 18

The next morning, I waited until Sam left for her office before coming downstairs. I tried to be a considerate houseguest and stay out of her way during her morning routine. Plus, I really didn't want her trying to talk me into going running with her before the sun was even up. In the kitchen, I felt the side of the insulated coffee carafe, then peeked inside. *Awesome! She left a half pot of coffee for me and it's still warm.*

"Elmer? Are you here? Can you hear me?" I asked the empty house. Nothing. I looked around, starting to get used to him just showing up behind me when I called him and scaring the crap out of me. Still no answer.

Jake came bounding into the room at the sound of my voice. Over the last couple days, he seemed to have transformed into a much younger dog. He looked so happy to have a dog friend to play with who could also see him. When they were together, the two of them looked just like two regular dogs, rather than one real and one ghost dog. Today I was going to have to pay attention more closely whenever they were side-by-side. I thought I had noticed slight differences the last time they played. I had focused on those differences, knowing I needed to be able to tell the difference between the living and ghosts more quickly, rather than just waiting to see if someone or something passed through them or not. Those two were perfect guinea pigs.

The only way I could think of to describe it was to compare the difference between a good quality high resolution digital picture and a low resolution one after they've been blown up larger. They're a little grainy, the colors are less distinct, and less solid looking. That's kind of what Jake looked like compared to Toby. I guess if that was the most obvious difference between the two dogs then maybe it would be true for other ghost situations, too.

"What are you doing?" came from right behind me.

I jumped and whirled around to face him. "Seriously Elmer?"

"What?"

"Do *all* ghosts get some kind of obscene pleasure from making the living nearly wet themselves, or am I just lucky that the first two I've met are into it?"

"Oh. Sorry. No. I'll try to be more aware of that."

"Thank you!"

"But again . . . what are you doing?" he asked.

"I was comparing the differences between Toby and Jake's appearances when they were playing. Today I want to see if I can figure those differences out and how I can work with them. So I can hopefully avoid unpleasant surprises in the future."

"Oh, okay. You appeared frozen. You didn't move a muscle for the entire three minutes I've been standing here. I was afraid something was wrong."

"Can any ghost see any other ghost? Is it easy for you to tell the difference?" I asked curiously.

"Yes, as far as I know. It should get easier for you to tell the difference with time, too."

I explained what I had noticed so far to him. "Will you call Jake to you for a sec?"

Before he had a chance to do so, Jake jumped up and put his front feet on Elmer. I eyed him suspiciously. I still believed he could understand me.

I turned my attention back to Elmer. "So, ghosts can touch ghosts as if they're both solid then?"

"Well, sort of, but not exactly," he answered. "We're both at the same—density level, I guess you might call it—right now, so he can do that. If I went in either other direction, he wouldn't be able to."

"What do you mean?"

Elmer looked up at the ceiling, thinking. "I should have known you would ask that, curious girl! Let's see. How about I start with when I disappear? I'm not always gone. Sometimes I'm 'gray'. My natural state as a ghost, spirit, or whatever, is a really small speck of dim gray light. You probably can't even see me with your naked eyes, and by *you,* I mean someone with the Sight. That takes the least amount of effort and drains the least amount of my energy to maintain, so unless I want you to be able to see me, that's how I stay. Doing this, being visible for you, isn't too bad. To increase my density enough so I can touch you, though, is very draining."

"Rand mentioned that. Which reminds me—when your energy gets drained—how do you get it back?" Something else he said hit me. "Wait. So, all those times I called for you, you were just ignoring me?"

"No, not always," he hedged, before continuing. "Sometimes if our energy drops too low, we kind of go into a hibernation mode. But our energy, it just—gradually comes back. I'm not sure how else to explain it. Like osmosis or something? Everything is made of energy and occupies space. If any one thing has less energy than everything around it, it kind of absorbs energy from everything else until they're all even. Does that make sense?"

"I think so." I decided to ignore that 'not always.' For now.

"Say, for instance, I had run over to your house that day instead of sending Jake. I may not have even had the energy left to make myself visible for you afterwards. Possibly not even the next day. It took me a while to learn to balance all that," he explained.

"Okay, I get it. Is that where you were when I called you a few minutes ago?"

"Yes and no. I was in that gray space, but I was upstairs in the attic again."

That immediately worried me. "What? Why?"

"I was just looking at some old pictures of Birdie and I," he said sadly.

Oh. Not sure how to respond to the sudden change in his mood, I hoped maybe a trip to the park would cheer him back up again.

"I'm going down to the park to see Rand. Would you like to come? I thought Jake and Toby could play again. It's a really nice day out," I coaxed.

I had to get up. Sitting on these bar stools for very long tended to make my legs fall asleep. I took my coffee cup over to the sink, rinsed it, and put it in the dishwasher.

"I don't think I will today, Roxie. You and Jake go ahead. I'd make for poor company I'm afraid."

"You want me to stay home instead? I can go another time—"

"No, no. You run along now. It's okay. I'll be here when you get back."

"Okay then . . . if you're sure."

"I am. Now go take Jake to see Toby. He'll enjoy the time with his friend!"

***

I felt kind of guilty, but Jake was eager to go, so we walked down to the park together to meet Rand and Toby. They were already there when we got there. As soon as the two dogs got near one another, it was easy to confirm my earlier thoughts. I found that I could *easily* tell the difference now between a spirit and a living creature.

After giving Toby an ear rub and greeting Rand, I got right down to business. "What do you know about magical rings and jewelry?" I asked him, trying to sound casual.

"*What* kind of rings?"

"Magical rings, possibly spelled. You know—ones with spells cast on them?"

"Nothing, sorry. Why do you ask?" he wanted to know, curious now.

It dawned on me that Rand had not been a ghost for a long time, but he still knew more about the paranormal world than me. Maybe he would be helpful when I got a chance to start reading the books and journals Elmer gave me. I knew I needed to spend more time learning about this world that hadn't even existed for me two months ago.

Should I tell Rand about the journals and stuff? Should I wait until I know him a little better? I can trust him by now, right?

"Oh, I ran across something about magical rings and some other, um, stuff, that mentioned those of us with the Sight being able to See into the shadow world. I wondered if you would be interested in researching that with me some time?" I asked.

"Yeah, sure! We spirits have the same Sight as you, as far as I know. Getting more training on anything to do with that sounds good to me."

I let out a breath I hadn't even realized I was holding. *At least there are still guys around that will admit they don't know everything! Steven would have just BS'd his way through.*

"How would *you* define the shadow world?" I asked him, walking back to my seat.

He got up and walked a couple of steps away, and then looked back at me thoughtfully. "There's a world of light on the other side of the portal between here and there that we spirits just call 'the light,' so to me everything on this side of the portal is the shadow world."

I sat back down slowly. "I guess I'm having trouble understanding what you just said. Everybody's heard about the light, and crossing over. Where do you cross over *to*? And your definition of the shadow world sounds just exactly like what I call the regular world . . . "

Rand shot me a grin as he shook his head, thinking, before he tried again. "The light comes from a different—dimension. Only the light, pure energy, and thought exist there. Nothing physical. Time doesn't even exist there. When any living creature here dies, its spirit rises out of the body and finds itself in an unnatural, somewhat uncomfortable surrounding. Probably similar to what a baby experiences at birth.

"The light shining through the portal offers to let the spirit cross to a place that suits it better, you might say. The urge to do that is really strong."

He thought for a moment before going on. "Now some spirits, for whatever reason, aren't offered the light. They're pretty much stuck here, in an uncomfortable state. Some take that ok, and some get pretty pissed off about it. There are also quite a few like me, who resist the light while we try to deal with something really important to us here before we go. I have noticed though, that the longer I resist it, the less uncomfortable I feel."

"Thank you. I think I kind of get it."

We just watched quietly for a while as Toby and Jake ran around, playing and getting better acquainted. It was obvious that they were already great friends. Though what others must think, seeing Toby acting that way supposedly by himself!

"Do many dogs—er, animals have the Sight like Toby does?" I asked.

"A lot more animals than people do, yes. I don't know how many exactly. But most animals can sense spirits, even if they can't see them."

We were out of the wind on my favorite bench, and the sun was shining. It was a very beautiful day. "This would be a perfect place to just enjoy the sun and read a book, if I didn't have so many things going on all at once in my life."

"Tell me about it. Things kind of haven't worked out so good for me either," he deadpanned, "being as I'm dead and all."

"Okay, you definitely win the 'woe is me' contest. I'm wondering if there's any upside to suddenly having the Sight, in my case. What do you think, Rand?"

"Depends a lot on you, I'd think. I'm not an expert on living beings with the Sight, but I am living it as a spirit. I'm like the Invisible Man without the need to eat or to own a home or a car anymore. I have no use for money, because I have no way to spend it, nor anything to spend it on. So, I don't need a job. I do however have the desire to be seen, so when I discovered that you could see me, I was instantly drawn to you. I'd imagine that's true for lots of spirits. Look at Jake. He definitely likes Toby being able to see him, and you too. Seems like there'd be a lot of ways for you to cash in on that, if you had a mind to. On the other hand, I imagine there are spirits and Others that would *not* appreciate the fact that you can see them. It takes away their freedom of invisibility and anonymity around you."

"What do you mean?" I asked.

"Well, there are far more Others out there than there are spirits. They look just like anyone else to the living. Why? Because that's what people's conscious minds *want* them to see.

Then along comes you. A witch may look like a regular person to most, but they'll stand out like a sore thumb to you. Your gut—or maybe your magick—will tell you they're Other. They wear a glamour, of sorts. Trust me when I say you don't want a witch noticing that you know she's more than she appears. Your best defense will be keeping a poker face and acting like you didn't while moving as far away from her as you can.

"There are more shifters out there than anything as far as paranormal beings go. They'll look just like anybody else to a normal person while in their human form. To you and I they'll look like one of those apps where you can morph an animal's face on a human head and body. Again, poker-face. We're a threat to their anonymity. There's generally not much they can do to me. I can just ghost out and disappear. You can't do that. They might want to eliminate you as a threat just for noticing them."

"I don't have a good poker face. I'm more of a scream and get out of dodge type," I admitted. I remembered what Elmer had told me about witches and ghosts. Was it possible Rand just didn't know what witches could do to him?

"Then—we need to work on that, ASAP," Rand continued.

I picked up my notebook and started taking notes.

"What else is out there?" I asked.

"Vampires, demons, the fae . . . There are probably more I haven't encountered. Unfortunately, I don't exactly have any kind of network for intel these days."

I wasn't sure I liked where this conversation had gone. "And I suppose they all look like regular people *to* regular people, right?"

"Yep. To you, a vampire will look just like anyone else, except for his teeth, of course. You'll still know one when you see it though, like with a witch. You'll feel it. That's the only way to describe it. And that's assuming it's the same for you as it is for me. Demons can look like anything they want to, from an animal to a human child, to something extremely gross and terrifying. Their choice. But, again, you'll know them right off. They don't ever actually touch the ground. I don't think they physically can.

"Oh, then there's the aliens. I know of at least two kinds. The reptilian ones, and the gray ones. They both look like regular people *to* regular people, of course. To you and I, the grays will look like small, skinny human children with of course gray skin and heads slightly too big for their bodies just like the ones portrayed in those Roswell films. The reptilian type will be really tall, muscular, and well—reptilian."

"Aliens?" my voice was little more than a squeak by now. "Are you serious?"

"No. That last bit I made up," he laughed. "But just because I've never seen one doesn't mean they're not out there. It's a big world."

If I could have, I would have punched him.

Chapter 19

"Why don't we go somewhere public, somewhere with a lot of people and see what we can see?" Rand suggested. "I think you're due for an eye opener."

It was getting chilly, as dusk wasn't far away now so we decided to move the conversation indoors. Sam was going to be late tonight, and I didn't feel like cooking. "What if we just go to the Sagebrush Cantina, sit at the bar, order some Mexican take-out, and wait until it's ready? I don't feel like actually going out for the evening yet. Can you do that?" I asked.

"Sure I can. That place should work. I haven't been there in a long time, but I can't imagine it's changed too awful much. As long as you can drive, and then drop me off at the van after. That's where Toby lives with *that woman*. In her van. I know all her usual parking places."

"What do you mean by 'parking places'?"

"She stealth parks on the streets in the more industrial areas. Her van doesn't look like a camper on the outside, so nobody suspects. But it has everything inside. Parking's free that way. She has solar on the roof, so she doesn't need to plug in anywhere. She has a membership at a fitness club that she only uses for the showers and bathrooms."

"I think I've actually heard of that. And yes, I can drop you off, after. Do you really think we'll see anything in a small town like Fenton, on a Thursday evening?" I asked, curious.

"Um, yeah? They're everywhere. They live here, same as you. Some of them need to eat, same as you. Others just want to be around people—for good reasons or bad, but that doesn't matter to us. You just need some experience spotting them—and maintaining that poker-face."

**

To say that Rand was right would be such an understatement. I had no sooner walked through the second set of doors of the entry airlock at Sagebrush Cantina and gave my eyes a moment to get used to the lower light levels, when I saw two young guys sitting with two pretty girls at a table dead-center in the middle of the room—with dog faces. One looked like a hound, complete with floppy ears, the other appeared to be a husky of some sort. I remembered Rand's warning and kept my facial expression normal and my eyes straight ahead. I walked directly past them and to the far side of the room where the bar was, taking a stool all the way to the left, closest to the kitchen entrance. The worst place to sit, intentionally, so it would be less likely for someone else to come sit next to me.

The woman behind the bar came over to me, giving the counter a quick wipe and setting a napkin in the wet spot. I bit my tongue and reached over for a dry napkin.

"What can I get you, Hun?" she asked.

"Hi," I said, smiling at her. "I'd like two orders of Botana to go, and a strawberry margarita while I wait, please."

"Sure thing," she said, snapping her gum and moving along to get the food order in first.

As planned, I took out my phone and acted like I was talking to a friend on it so I could talk with Rand without drawing attention to myself. I had my back to the room, but there was a full-wall mirror right in front of me behind all the liquor bottles.

The bartender returned with my margarita, giving me an appreciative nod when I included a nice tip. Maybe next time I could get a dry napkin. Sipping my drink, I relaxed my shoulders and tried to look casual.

"Did you see the two dog-shifters as we came in?" Rand asked.

I laughed, finding them in the mirror. "Why yes! Yes I did, thank you," I said into the phone held to my ear. "How could I have missed—it?"

"I wasn't sure you did. You never even flinched! Good job with the poker face." Rand stood right next to me, leaning casually against the bar with his butt, facing directly their way.

"Obvious much?" I asked him. "You're going to give us away."

"Oh, don't worry, they can't see me. They aren't spirits; they're living beings." Then he turned around and sat down beside me suddenly.

"I see what you mean," I murmured quietly into the phone. "They're almost like—what do you call them—holographic images on a bookmark. They turn one way and look like a young man, turn the other way and look like a dog. It kind of makes my stomach flip a little."

"Behind them, way in the opposite corner of the room standing in front of the booth. Do you see the guy? The spirit?"

"Yes, I do," I said into the phone. "He's totally creeping on those girls sitting in the booth. It's hard to believe they can't tell he's there. I can't believe how bold he is!"

"As far as he knows, he's the Invisible Man. See what I told you? See how his gaze goes from face to face with who's speaking? He's really intent on their conversation. Look! He's leaning on the table so he can hear over the noise! He's not creeping on them, he's flat-out spying on them and he has no idea that anyone in the place can see him. He's a newbie."

Somebody new came through the door. A young woman—with a fluffy red fox face! She waved casually at the dog-shifter guys as she joined a table of human women.

"They obviously know each other. Can they see each other for what they truly are?" I asked into my phone.

"Yes, and they're no threat to each other, so they don't care."

"Where are their tails?" I asked, as the thought hit me completely out of the blue.

Rand chuckled quietly. "Down one pant leg, of course," he answered.

"Even the women? That's weird. And probably really uncomfortable. Please tell me this is another joke, like with the aliens."

He just smiled and shrugged. "Shifters are living beings. Unlike me, they need to eat, have a car, have families, and have a place to live. So, they need money. That means most of the younger ones need a job. Those are obviously the girls she works with—wherever."

"Younger ones?"

"Shifters age differently than normal humans. They can live for a very long time. Hundreds of years, easily. But they're mortal, meaning they can also die. Just not as easily. They heal really fast too. They can survive some pretty awful things, and then heal perfectly enough that you can't even tell. So, I'd say the majority of them, after enough time, get wealthy enough that they don't need to work. They just appear—retired."

"I guess that makes sense." I finished my drink with one large gulp, thinking I might need another one.

"Here comes your food," he warned.

I said good-bye to my phone and put it away as the bartender sat two plastic bags on the bar along with my bill. "That'll be $20.72" she said. "The big one is your hot food, the small one is your cold items and sauces."

I paid her, told her to keep the change, and I walked right out of the place without turning my head.

"You have an excellent poker-face. I don't know what you were talking about earlier," Rand told me as we crossed the parking lot in the dark.

We walked up to my car. I opened my door and climbed in. Rand went to the passenger side and got in without even opening the door. I shuddered. *Why does that mess with my head just a little? He is a freaking ghost after all . . .*

"So, all my life there's been paranormals all around me—all around everyone, and we just couldn't see them!" I said, as we pulled out into traffic. "I can imagine some pretty creepy scenarios with that."

"There are creepy scenarios with anything. Try not to dwell on them."

"So, how does it work with those two shifter guys? Do they change into their kind of dog during the full moon, or what?"

Rand laughed. Hard. Until it started to tick me off. "That's just in the movies Roxie, sorry. It just struck me as funny. The answer is—they can shift any time they want into their animal form. Some of them, but not too many as far as I know, have a choice between two animal forms they can change into."

We saw a dead deer on the side of the road in the headlights. "Take that carcass we just passed, as an example. When it got hit by the car or whatever it was that killed it, if I happened to be standing right there, would I have seen its spirit leave its body?"

"Absolutely. It's the same with all living beings. Plants now, I have no idea, but squirrels, birds, deer, dogs, cats and the like— all have spirits. They all get offered their own light, so far as I know. I can't really imagine an evil animal. They operate on instinct. Humans are the only ones I know of who know right from wrong, and still choose wrong things sometimes," Rand said.

"Well Rand, thank you for this. It's definitely given me a lot to think about. Probably too much, in fact."

We found the white van at the second location we tried. I just pulled up down the street a bit from it momentarily and Rand disappeared right beside me as I watched. I shook my head, still barely able to believe that this was my life now.

***

I pulled into Sam's driveway just as she was getting out of her Cadillac inside the garage. *I wonder what she'd think if I told her what I just saw?*

"What's that?" Sam asked from inside the garage as she waited for me to follow her inside. She nodded at my bags. "You went out! Good for you!"

"Botanas, Chica! From Sagebrush. How was your day?" I followed her through the laundry room to the kitchen. I was still trying to figure out when and how to tell her about everything, including dog shifters, of all things, but she started telling me about her day as we sat and worked our way through the two giant trays of exquisite Mexican cuisine, and the time just wasn't right.

Chapter 20

For the past week, I'd been dying for pizza. And there was nothing quite as good as a homemade pizza, especially on a Friday night. Pulling out everything I needed to make one from scratch, I got to work. While the dough was rising, I prepared the sauce. As I had learned from my mother, *nothing* beat homemade pizza sauce. Season, simmer, taste, then repeat until it was perfect. That and there could never be too much cheese on a pizza. I couldn't find any pepperoni but there was deli ham in the fridge, along with fresh pineapple chunks. Hawaiian pizza it was.

For almost the next half hour I lost myself to the rhythm of punching down the dough, kneading it again lightly, rolling it out to fit the pan and letting it rise again on it. I layered on the sauce and toppings and had only just popped it in the oven, when I heard Sam come through the door from the garage.

"Roxie is that smell what I think it is?" she stopped in the kitchen, closing her eyes, and inhaling deeply.

I laughed, "That would depend on what you think it is."

Opening her eyes, she looked over at the mess piled in the sink and smiled. "What kind?"

"Hawaiian. With lots and lots of pineapple."

"I know I've asked you this before, but will you marry me?"

"We've discussed this. Neither of us are into women, remember?" I bantered back, laughing at her. It was a joke we'd had ever since we started hanging out together outside of the office. The first time she tasted one of my homemade deep-dish pizzas was on an evening we were prepping for a huge case. She'd apparently never had pizza that wasn't from a box, a freezer, or a drive-through. Her mock proposal had thrown me for a loop, so I had laughingly responded that I really wasn't into women then, too. When she'd tasted my spaghetti, with sauce that had simmered most of the day, I actually began to worry she was going to take me shopping for a ring. After that, it took me nearly two months before I dared to make manicotti with red wine tomato sauce and invite her over.

"I will totally switch sides. Just until I can find a man that can cook like you do, anyway."

"You used to date a guy that could cook. You said he had too much baggage, remember? Maybe Dr. Lane can cook. You should ask him out sometime."

She blushed a bit at the mention of the doctor who had handled my head injury. "Maybe I will. Hey, you think you can teach him to make sauce like you do? Because if you can—I may actually propose to him instead of you."

"Please do. My divorce isn't even final yet!"

That thought sobered us both for a moment. But only until the oven beeped, signaling us that the pizza was ready.

As we sat eating pizza that oozed cheese with every bite, we reviewed everything that had been happening in mediation and what I could expect at the upcoming mediation we would all be attending. If I was lucky, it would be the final meeting and the divorce would pretty much be a done deal, pending a Judge's signature.

"What about the jewelry, Sam? Will he have it there?"

"He's supposed to. Make sure you bring your set of keys to the Camaro for the exchange, he's adamant that he gets to keep the car."

"They're already in my purse. And he can keep that car! I never liked it to begin with. Are we really almost finished with this mess?"

"We are, Rox. You're holding up pretty well so far, I have to say," she eyed me thoughtfully.

"Well, it helps when I have a rockstar lawyer, who is also a rockstar friend." We both laughed at that.

"So," she continued, as she stood to clear away the plates, "now that that's settled, I'll clean up here in the kitchen, and then we can talk about boys!"

Laughing, "How about *we* clean up in the kitchen, since I made this huge mess, then I'll put on a fresh pot of coffee and we'll talk about boys."

"Ooh. Coffee. Who cares about boys?" she laughed.

***

Early the next morning, Sam and I took the Jeep over to my house, planning to load it up with as much as it would hold. Tess and Annie were going to join us in an hour or so, giving us time to take 'before' pictures of the house. Tess was bringing totes and boxes left from a recent move.

I deactivated the security system while Sam took a quick walk around the house to make sure everything was undisturbed and to take pictures with her phone. I went inside and started taking pictures of each room from different angles, using my phone. Shaking my head, I was still amazed by these little smart phones and how we could barely function without them anymore.

"You should use video for this part."

I jumped when Sam spoke from right behind me, nearly dropping my phone. "Give a girl some warning next time!"

Laughing, she looked around. "Tell you what. How about I do the video walk-through. You can go behind me and open some windows to get the mustiness out. Then we can start cataloging what's what and whether you want to keep anything here, sell it with the house, or whatever."

Both of us got to work. Before we knew it Tess and Annie arrived, each carrying in an armload of totes. Annie set hers down first and I saw her shirt. It read 'Um . . . Nope' on the front. She turned and I laughed as I read the back . . . 'Still Nope'. I loved her shirts.

"Hey Girls! I figured we could use these first. If we need them I'll bring the boxes in later," Tess said, setting the totes in the middle of the living room. "Where's the coffee? I've only been up for about an hour."

Sam and I looked at each other and cracked up. Tess was always straight to the point. That's why we loved her. The woman absolutely ran on coffee. If it would have been possible to put it in an I.V. bag to port it into her bloodstream faster, she would have done it—with a cup of coffee in her hand at the same time.

"I'll go put a pot on right now."

"And, hey. Who are the two old people across the street? They were eyeballing us like we were going to come in and rob you."

Sam rushed to the front door. "The Delaney's! I should have warned them. I'll be right back."

As I filled the carafe with water and prepped the coffee pot, Annie strode into the kitchen. "Where do you want me to start?"

"Oh, um, how about just a general wipe down for the surfaces first, then we'll figure everything else out. I'll tackle the fridge—I know it has to be bad in there. It hasn't even been open in what, five weeks now?"

"The power is on. It shouldn't be that bad," she said, opening the fridge door. "Eh. I've seen worse. Way worse. I'll grab a garbage bag and just toss anything that's expired or iffy." She grabbed the box of garbage bags from where I directed her and got right to work. Yes, I had awesome friends.

The coffee was done in minutes. As soon as we each grabbed a cup we got back to what we were doing. I couldn't believe the creamer was still good. *What the heck kind of chemicals did they put in there?*

Tess was tackling the dining room, packing up my mother's china from the china cabinet. She had thought to bring packing materials, thank goodness. Sam had gone upstairs with a couple totes and was going to work on clearing one of my dressers. I had already packed up most of my closet, using two of the suitcases from the set Steven and I had splurged on a few years ago for a vacation. I filled the other two with his stuff. Everything else of his was going into either boxes or garbage bags. I brought both of his suitcases downstairs to take out to the garage, figuring I would store all of his stuff in there for now. I paused long enough to grab a bottle of water from the now sparkling refrigerator.

"Wow, Annie. I don't think it was this clean when it was new." The woman was amazing.

She smiled and pointed to the pantry. "What about all of the foodstuff?"

I knew what it looked like in there. Steven had always insisted I keep it well-stocked. "If there's anything you can use, take it. I may take some things to Sam's—in fact, you know what she has and what she doesn't, since you shop for her. Why don't you take anything that you know she uses and set it aside? We'll take it back with us tonight if there's room left in the Jeep."

She chewed her lip for a moment. "Are you sure? Won't you use any of this?"

"I am absolutely sure. This house is going to sit empty for who knows how long. That stuff will just end up expiring. If you don't want it, it goes to the Food Bank."

She nodded and I let out a mental sigh of relief. She worked harder than anyone else I knew. If she could use any of the food, I was more than glad to give it.

"I'm going to take one of the totes out to the Jeep and then figure out what to do with Steven's things. Holler if you need anything."

I went back into the living room, grabbing the tote, and headed toward the front door. Before I had quite made it there, the second to the last person I ever wanted to see again stepped in. Michelle.

She looked around the room, taking in the totes and Steven's two suitcases sitting near the door. Her glare returned to me. "What are you doing?"

I made a show of looking around, as she had. "I'm packing."

"You can't take anything out of my dad's house!"

"I'm pretty sure I can take anything I want out of *my* house. My name is on the mortgage, too. In fact, the majority of the down payment was made by me."

"This is my dad's house, you hag! If you take one thing out of here, I'll call the police!"

Hag? Had she looked in the mirror lately? Her hair looked like she had just rolled out of bed. And I could see her dark roots and split ends from here. She actually looked a bit . . . rough. Her appearance had always been more important to her than anything else. Maybe her dad being in jail had affected her pretty badly. I immediately began to feel sorry for her.

"Listen, Michelle. I know we haven't always gotten along. But what your dad did to me was wrong. I was in the hospital for weeks with my jaw wired shut."

She put her hand on her hip, thrusting her chin up. "Too bad it's not still wired shut. And my dad didn't do that to you. He said your clumsy ass tripped, and you fell out by the pool."

Why you little . . .

Sighing, I tried again. "Then why did he run, Michelle? Why did the police arrest him? Why did the neighbors hear him yelling at me and feel the need to call the police?"

"Because you're a lying bitch, that's why! You told the cops he hit you when he didn't, just because you—"

I snapped my hand up. "Stop right there, Michelle. You've never listened to me, but you *are* going to listen today. When Steven hit me, I was knocked unconscious. I couldn't have talked to the cops if I had wanted to. I was in a coma—a *coma*—for a week. I couldn't communicate with anybody, let alone the police, for almost two weeks. Your dad was already in jail by then. Whatever he told you? He lied. I have never, *ever* lied to you. Not once. You have done *nothing* but disrespect me from the moment you walked into my life. I never tried to take the place of your mom. I did my best to make you feel wanted here. I always tried to do right by you." At this point I was counting off on my fingers to her. But it felt so good to get this all out. "And you? You treated me like I was your maid, when you deigned to even acknowledge me. You took and took, without so much as a thank you."

She stared at me, stunned. Her lower lip wobbled a bit. Then . . . "BRAD! Get in here."

Pencil neck, I mean Brad, quickly stepped in behind her, looking like he would rather be anyplace but here. "H-Hi, Mrs. Bell." Michelle smacked his arm, not even looking back at him.

"How *dare* you speak to me that way. My dad's attorney is going to chew you up and spit you out. You won't have a bowl to piss in when he—"

"Pot, Michelle. It's a *pot* to piss in. What exactly *did* you learn at that expensive college?" I asked, crossing my arms and leaning on the foyer wall.

I've always wondered what 'spitting fire' looked like. From the look in her eyes, I was probably going to find out.

"You get out of this house, *right now*. Brad—make her leave!" she demanded, smacking his arm again and gesturing at me. I looked at him with my eyebrows up.

"W-What? I-I don't think—"

I seriously felt sorry for the poor boy.

"Oh, dammit Brad, just get her out of here!" Michelle ordered.

His mouth moved, but no sounds came out this time. He reminded me a bit of a goldfish. He backed up a few steps, out onto the porch landing.

Michelle made a sound of disgust and then latched onto my arm, pulling me toward the door. I outweighed her by at least thirty pounds, so she had to work at it. I was still considering how hard I wanted to make it for her when Sam spoke up from the top of the stairwell.

"That. Is. Enough, Michelle Bell. Remove your hands from my client this instant. You have exactly five seconds to vacate these premises before I call the police."

"You can't make me. This is my dad's house!" she screeched.

"I can make you—or rather the police can—and I have everything you just said and did recorded. Smile for the camera." She angled her phone up so Michelle would see it better. "I can just as easily get a Personal Protection Order served against you, as I did your father. Take your hands off my client and leave. Now!"

There were few who could stand up to Samantha Stone when she used that tone of voice. Heck, I almost turned to leave.

Michelle released my arm and took a couple steps back. "This isn't—"

"Oh, for crying out loud, Michelle. If you say, 'this isn't over', I'm calling the Cliche Police. Now get out of my house."

The half-second of confusion that crossed her expression was replaced instantly with rage. She paused to look around the small foyer, snatching the small vase of artificial flowers that sat on the entry table. She launched them at me, then turned to bolt out the door. Reflexively, I threw my hands up to protect my face and I felt a—push of energy, just as she opened the door. Somehow the vase that had been coming straight at me missed, hitting the wall just inches from my head. She flew over the two front steps, landing hard on the sidewalk. As Brad helped her up, she shot me a look of pure venom.

Shocked, I still managed to call out after her, "You always sucked at sports!" And then I collapsed to the floor.

Sam rushed down the stairs, but Annie and Tess reached me first. "Are you okay?" Annie's eyes were huge. Tess looked angry.

"I'm fine. Really," I insisted, as they helped me up off the floor. I suddenly—felt better.

Sam shook her head. "I don't think that's the last we'll see of her. Or should I say that *you'll* see of her." She held up her phone. "But this will help."

Sighing, I knew she was right. Michelle would be a problem.

We quickly finished packing up as much as possible and called it a day. Annie and Tess would meet us back here tomorrow to finish up. Steven's clothing and personal items would be boxed up and stored in the garage until I contacted a storage facility. Most of the things I wanted to keep were already packed up in the back of my Jeep.

Chapter 21

Wednesday morning found us in the mediations room at the courthouse. I was so not ready for this. I wore both the opal pendant and the little black ring as a precaution, remembering Rosemary's warnings. The Power Ring was in my purse, simply because I wasn't used to wearing so much jewelry, but I wanted it close.

We arrived far earlier than our appointment time. Sam has always had a thing about never being late. Her motto went way beyond the usual 'if you're not ten minutes early, consider yourself late' saying. Hers was more like 'twenty minutes early. Period'. We settled in to wait for Steven and his attorney and went over everything one more time. By the time they arrived—five minutes late—I almost felt like I could do this.

For a good hour, Sam and the other attorney—Isaac B. Holden, his business card read—went over every asset we had accumulated over the past ten years. Sam was going for an equitable division of assets, which I had agreed was fair enough. I listened, studying Steven's attorney while Steven stared at me, scowling. Mr. Holden was probably close to our age and wore an expensive looking suit and tie but, other than that, was fairly nondescript. Brownish hair, pale blue eyes, average height, and a face that was neither attractive nor ugly. In short, he was—unmemorable.

By contrast, Steven looked . . . rough. And not in a good way—his eyes were bloodshot, he needed a shave, and his hair was unkempt. He had on a suit as well, but it was ill-fitting. I don't think I had ever seen him like this before. I hadn't seen him carry anything in with him, so I wondered where my jewelry was.

Steven's glare was starting to get to me. His attorney must have advised him to remain quiet and let him do the negotiating. I was just shocked that he had listened. Steven absolutely hated being told what to do. Just as I was going to ask if we could take a break, he spoke up. Both Sam and Steven's lawyer turned to look at us.

"Come on, Roxie, you don't really want this, do you? Listen to all of this. We built a good life together. We should work through it. You know, go to some counseling or something. I was going to say something when I saw you—you look really good. Did you lose weight? There's no need for all of this," he motioned to the two attorneys. His wheedling voice was at odds with the scowl on his face.

Stunned, I didn't know what to say. Under the table, Sam grabbed my hand and gave a reassuring squeeze.

Sam raised a brow at my soon-to-be ex-husband. "Mr. Bell, you assaulted my client and put her in the hospital for three weeks. You then fled the scene, leaving her bleeding next to the pool. I have both the police and the hospital records with me if we need to refresh your memory. She had bleeding on the brain and was in a coma for a week. You left her with a broken jaw.

They had to put in plates and screws to put it back together. Counseling can't fix that."

Steven turned his glare to Sam, as his attorney leaned back and watched with interest. "You. This is your fault. You put these ideas into her head!" he spat at her. "I hardly touched her! She fell!"

I couldn't remain quiet any longer. "Steven Bell! You punched me in the face hard enough to knock me down. You nearly killed me! I remember everything. I remember the murder in your eyes. I even remember you spitting all over me while you yelled at me. Most of all, I remember the fear and the pain. I will *always* remember that. We haven't been happy for a long time, Steven. I haven't been able to do or say anything to make you happy for years. I'm tired, Steven. I'm tired of what I want, never mattering, of everything being about you. I'm tired of giving up every little piece of myself, just because you think I should be at your beck and call. I'm done with that. You either agree to what's on the table now or I'll go after absolutely everything."

Sam turned to me during my outburst. I ignored her as she wiped a fake tear from her eye and put her hand to her chest like a proud mother. Somehow, I managed not to roll my eyes. Steven's lawyer just frowned at us both.

"You can't do that!" my soon-to-be-ex hissed at me. Turning to his attorney, "She can't do that, right? Tell her."

"I'm afraid she can, Steven. There's a small chance she might not win, but the deck *is* stacked heavily in her favor. If you want to fight this, it will be long and expensive. And you will probably end up paying her attorney fees if you lose," his lawyer replied evenly. He nodded toward Sam. "What Ms. Stone is proposing is pretty standard. Mrs. Bonacci-Bell will be awarded half of everything, including what the house sells for, in exchange for an uncontested divorce. It really could go much worse for you. And, according to this, she will drop the assault charges, though the PPO will remain in place."

"And my jewelry. I want the jewelry you took out of our safe, Steven," I threw in. "That was an inheritance that you don't have any right to. You were supposed to bring it."

He turned calculating eyes on me. "Fine. You can have that jewelry back, but I keep my Camaro."

I felt Sam nudge my foot twice. That was the signal we had worked out beforehand. It meant he was buckling and to just go with it. This was a small concession for it all being over and he would think he had come out ahead this way.

"Great. You keep the Camaro. I want my jewelry back. Now.

He jumped out of his seat. "You can have your stupid jewelry back."

Mr. Holden put a hand on Steven's arm to guide him back down to his seat. "Mr. Bell, please. We are almost finished here. Mrs. Bonacci-Bell, I have the envelope of jewelry your husband gave me outside the courthouse this morning, right here in my briefcase. There was some worry about bringing it through the metal detectors."

He reached down and pulled the envelope out, setting it on the table between us. I slid it over and opened it up, dumping the contents out in front of me. Frowning at the small pile, I recognized most of the jewelry I had purchased for myself or received from Steven over the years. I saw a few pieces that I vaguely remembered taking out of my mother's jewelry boxes but there seemed to be some missing.

I looked at Steven and asked flatly, "Where's the rest of it?"

"What are you talking about? That's everything!" he spat at me.

I pulled out my spare set of keys to the Camaro and held them up. "I will put miles on that car until I get *all* of it back. And I might not remember what kind of gas it takes, got me? I want every last piece back, Steven, I mean it."

He jumped out of his seat and reached into his pocket. "Take your stupid jewelry back, it's not even worth enough money to bother with!" He threw a handful of rings and pendants across the table at me. None hit me, but several fell into my lap or onto the floor. Calmly leaning over to pick the ones on the floor up, I had a sudden flash of intuition just as my fingers brushed the last piece I was reaching for.

I narrowed my eyes at Steven as I straightened. "And the pendant in your other pocket?"

His face went slack with astonishment. He sputtered for a moment before reaching into his other pocket and pulling out the pendant I had somehow seen for the briefest moment in my mind. I would worry about what that was about later, for now I made sure I held his gaze and didn't show any emotion on my face. I fully expected him to throw it at me, but he set it firmly down right in front of me. His glare held nothing but hatred in it as I swept all of the jewelry into the envelope.

Mr. Holden put a hand on Steven's arm to guide him back down to his seat, frowning disapprovingly at either his client's display or his dishonesty. Or perhaps both. "Mr. Bell, please. We are almost finished here."

'Almost finished' ended up being another hour of paperwork, signatures, and more paperwork. Steven sat with his arms crossed, alternating between glaring at me and pouting. I tried to focus on just getting through the mound of papers so we could get out of there. By the last signature, I wasn't even sure what I was signing, but I trusted Sam implicitly. Just before we stood to leave the mediation room, I slid the car keys over to Steven and left the room just ahead of Sam.

When we finally walked out of the courthouse it was well after noon. I had the envelope of jewelry tucked safely in my purse. Sam and I decided to grab take-out for her whole office from Hoffman's Deco Deli and Cafe.

Tess was the first to jump up and grab some of the bags we were carrying in and head off to the break room. We met her and the rest of the staff there.

"Well?" she asked, already diving into the food. "How did it go? Did you make that butt-head pay?"

"I think we're both walking away with what's fair," I said quietly.

Sam looked over at me sharply. "Hardly! After what he did to you and the crap you've taken from him for years, he's lucky to walk away with anything! But I was really proud of you, there, Rox. You stood up for yourself. I haven't seen you do that in—I can't even remember how long. Not with him, anyway."

I let out a shaky breath. "I'm just glad it's over. Another couple of weeks and the divorce will be final and I'll . . . ," I paused, not able to go on.

"Uh-oh," Tess said as she jumped up and wrapped her arms around me. "It's hitting her. Want to give her some good news?"

Sam joined her, hugging an arm around both of us. "Yeah, I may have forgotten to mention your final bill for the divorce."

"Um, what?" I couldn't believe she was bringing this up now.

"Yes, I wrote it into the agreement that both of you signed. Steven is paying for the whole divorce," she grinned. "And I may have charged slightly more than my normal going rate. And allowed for any future discrepancies."

Tess nodded, with a sly grin of her own. "I prepared the invoice myself. I'm pretty sure he's even paying for this lunch."

Laughing, I hugged them back and sat down to eat. I don't know what I would do without such great friends in my life.

Chapter 22

I paid Annie to do a thorough cleaning of the house and did the touch-up painting myself. All of this kept me so busy I didn't have the spare time or energy to pursue looking at any of the journals. The jewelry I had recovered still sat in the envelope in the nightstand, next to Elmer's box. I rarely even saw Elmer during any of that time. When I did, he seemed more distant than usual.

Two weeks later . .

"Shut the front door! Three-hundred-seventy-nine thousand dollars?! After only three days on the market? *Heck yes* I'll take it! Just show me where to sign, Sam!" I quickly did the math in my head. Minus realtor fees plus what was still owed, that would leave me with around $102,000. And then there was what we had in our savings and investments. I blew out a breath. Maybe things were going to be alright, after all.

"I'll go over the paperwork with my realtor friend and bring home the purchase agreement for you to sign tonight then. That's the first step. Next, we have to get Steven to sign it," she explained.

That last part burst my bubble completely. "Knowing him, he'll probably refuse to sign the papers. He'll be as big of a prick as he possibly can, guaranteed."

"Don't worry Rox, this won't be the first peeing-for-distance competition I've been involved in. His fragile ego is in for some rough treatment ahead, if he gets too cocky with us." Sam's smile was almost predatory, as if she was looking forward to the challenge.

I am so glad Sam's on my side.

"So, what happens now? What if he refuses and we lose the buyers?"

"Then we get a judge involved. And I guarantee that any judge in this county will be on your side, especially with an assault charge, even though you've agreed not to press charges now. This divorce agreement is already a done deal—the judge will see he's just dragging his feet. There's absolutely nothing he can do to stop this now, since the papers are signed. Think about it—you two have no children together, you were married almost—oh my gosh! Roxie, it would have been ten years, right after your birthday next month!"

"Yeah, I know. I've been trying not to think about it."

"The anniversary or your birthday?"

"Either! This is going to be the crappiest birthday ever."

"Not on my watch it's not, Rox. This is going to be a completely fresh start for you. Look at yourself," she stood up, pulling me with her, and spun me around to face the gilt-framed mirror hanging behind me. "Seriously girlfriend, look at yourself. You just lost all that marital weight—and I'm not just talking about the twenty pounds," I raised my brow at her reflection. "Look at all you have going for you. You are beautiful. You are smart. *And* you have a fabulous lawyer." We both laughed at that.

If only I could tell her about everything else I had *going for* me.

"Anyway," she continued, as we sat down again. "You are going to be just fine financially. You're even getting half of his pension. He earned most of that while you were married, so you are technically entitled to a portion of it, so don't you dare give me that guilty look, Roxanne Bonacci. When everything is said and done, you might not even have to go back to work for a while, you know. If you had let me ask for alimony, you wouldn't have had to think about work for a long time."

"What? I'll still have to find a place to live and housing isn't exactly cheap around here. I don't want anything to do with him past this divorce. I want to do *something*; I just don't know what. And Sam, I am really grateful that you're letting me stay here—I appreciate that, you know I do, but—"

"Roxie, you know you can stay with me as long as you want," she interrupted. "I absolutely love having you around. I never really noticed before how big this house was living here all alone." She made a sweeping motion with her arm, as if to prove her point.

I wasn't touching that last thing she said, yet. I still had no idea how to break it to her that she had never really lived here alone. "What if I paid rent or something? Just until I get back on my feet and figure things out."

"Absolutely not! Like I said, it's a good thing that you're here. And, if you get bored or we start to get on each other's nerves, we'll figure something out. Tell you what," she held up her hand to halt my protest. "We'll discuss all of that later. Now, can we get back to more important issues?"

"Of course, what else do we still need to go over?"

She smiled again, mischievously this time, "Help me pick out a dress. I've got a date tomorrow night!"

We both squealed like schoolgirls. "It's Leo, I mean Dr. Lane, isn't it?"

"Yes! We've been texting and talking since you got out of the hospital. He finally asked me out!"

"I want deets. I can't *believe* you haven't said a word about this to me."

She huffed on her nails and shined them on her shirt smugly, "Well, I thought he was a lot younger than what he is, so I didn't want to say anything until I kind of knew *if* I wanted it to go anywhere. And this is only a first date, so it might be nothing."

"Sam. It most certainly won't be 'nothing'. I could feel the chemistry between you two every single time he walked into my hospital room. He's perfect for you, I just know it!"

"But I don't usually have time for this. Dating. Getting to know someone. Most men are intimidated by my success. He's . . . different."

"That's because he's on your level. He knows you're busy and successful—he is too. You two couldn't be more right for each other. How old is he, by the way?"

"He's thirty-eight."

"For real? I *seriously* thought he was thirty-two at the most. Well, you only just turned forty-two, so there's barely an age gap at all. Sooo," I grinned at her. "Have you run a background check on him yet?" I already knew the answer.

"What do you think?" she deadpanned.

"Come on, Sam. Dirt. Please!" I gave her my best puppy dog eyes.

"There isn't any," she shrugged. "Like—nothing at all. No ex-wife, no child support payments, not so much as a parking ticket. He's nearly paid off his student loans. He's an absolutely brilliant doctor. From what I can see and what we've discussed, he's put one hundred percent of his focus into his work. And now he thinks he's ready for something—more than work."

I dipped my head as I stood up, letting my hair fall forward to hide my happy tears. She deserved this more than anyone I knew. She had dated on and off during the years we'd been friends but her natural confidence, as well as her success, drove many of her would-be suitors away. The rest could never pass her background check test. Leo seemed like a perfect match. Seeing her this excited, even when my life was such a mess, made me ecstatic for her. As much as I wanted to spend the evening going through my mother's jewelry, my friend needed me more. To be honest, doing something this normal felt really good.

Upstairs, we dissected most of her closet, eventually going for a classic little black dress. With her height, she rarely wore anything with a heel, but the black kitten heels we paired with the dress were too perfect to forego. As we went through her jewelry, I was reminded how unusual all of my 'new' jewelry was, compared to her more understated collection. In the end, we decided on a simple pair of earrings and a thin silver chain.

"Hair up or down?" she asked, as she pulled it up in front of the mirror.

"Definitely up. Your neck is a mile long. Show it off." I helped her pile it up, pinning it strategically so that a few errant strands framed her face. When I stood back and looked at her reflection in the mirror, she looked like a model, except ten times more elegant. With her slender runner's body, she didn't even need Spanx to hold anything in. If I didn't love her so much, I would be jealous.

"Roxie—I think I'm actually nervous!" Sam whispered.

"What? Samantha Stone, look at all you have going for you. You are beautiful. You are smart. *And* you are a fabulous lawyer. You have nothing to be nervous about." Throwing her pep talk from earlier back at her, I smiled as I hugged her. "Did I mention he's going to have to glue his eyes back in his head when he sees you? Now get out of that and put on some comfy clothes and let's go have coffee."

We laughed as we put everything away and headed back downstairs.

Chapter 23

As it turned out, Sam did have to take the matter to court and force the sale of the house. I had the remainder of Steven's things and most of the furniture I was moderately sure he would want to keep, put into a storage facility—one at the other end of town from mine. I made sure it was in his name and had Sam forward the information, including when the bill was due, to him through his lawyer.

"Guess what Elmer?" I announced, coming into the living room. "The sale of the house *and* the divorce proceedings are both final!"

"Well that was sure quick," he mumbled, like he was only half paying attention. He sat on the end of the sofa with Jake laying at his feet with his massive head up on Elmer's lap. He was petting Jake's fur and gently stroking his ears thoughtfully. Even the dog's ears were huge.

"Are you okay Elmer?" I asked, concerned with his expression.

"Yes, Roxanne, I am. I was just thinking of the day Birdie and I brought this big lug home to live with us. He was such a little guy then—well, compared to what he is now, anyway. Birdie carried him inside. Oh, if she could see him now—err, I mean while he was full grown. She never got to see that, you know? What Rosemary said has really got me to thinking." He lowered his head, his eyes getting moist.

I sat down beside him. "That's perfectly understandable and, no, I didn't know that Elmer. You haven't told me too much about your wife. I've been selfish and have only asked you questions about the Sight. But let's not even talk about that today. How about you tell me about the day you two brought Jake home? And some more days. Today, just tell me about Jake and Birdie."

He chuckled. "You better be careful what you ask for, young lady! I could keep you sitting here for a very long time on that topic."

"Well I have no place to be all afternoon. Tell me a story!"

Elmer leaned his head back, wiped at his eye, and smiled. "Heh! When we left to go get Jake from a farm out by Byron, Birdie had set some loaves of bread dough to rise on the dinner table with towels over them . . ."

"Oh no! He didn't."

Elmer had a bit of a laughing attack. "Oh yes he did! To this day I still don't know how he got up there. I didn't think this boy was gonna make it through his first day here. Come to think of it, I thought that most days. Seemed like Jake here terrorized my Birdie. She acted mad, but she was never mean to him. Nary a time. In fact, I saw her sneak him bits of our dinner many a time, shortly after threatening to beat him senseless. Nope. Birdie loved ole Jake just as much as I did. Didn't she boy?" He scruffed Jake's head and got a deep woof in reply.

He was right. Elmer had a ton of stories like that. As he shared them with me, his whole expression changed. He and Birdie had raised their children here. They'd seen wars come and go. They'd seen prosperous times and hard times as well, but when the kids were grown up and gone, their big house seemed empty. That's why they'd decided to get a dog—to fill that emptiness. It sounded like they were very happy here for a long time, until one day Birdie's doctor had some very bad news for them. She had cancer. It was too far along to treat, and she went quickly. Elmer was so devastated—an ocean of emptiness engulfed him. He really, really missed his wife.

I really wished I could give him a hug. The poor old guy. I never wanted to see Steven's face again as long as I lived, yet here was Elmer, heartbroken, wishing he could just see Birdie's face one more time. "We've talked about this before, Elmer. While I truly appreciate everything you've been teaching me, it breaks my heart how bad you're missing your wife. The promise still stands—if you want to cross over and be with her, I'll look after Jake for you. He seems to really like me, and it's not like he eats or makes messes. Wait—he *doesn't* eat—does he?" I asked.

Elmer looked at me thoughtfully. He scrunched his rather large, rounded nose and pushed his glasses up with one finger. Then he smiled. "No. He doesn't eat. Therefore, he doesn't have the need to eliminate waste, either. We're pure energy, Roxanne. All spirits are. The consciousness, or soul, of any living creature is best described as a spark of light and pure energy. You've heard the phrase 'from ashes to ashes and dust to dust', I'm sure. That's the physical body. It's more like 'from energy to energy and light to light' for the soul."

207

I thought about that for a moment. "You told me once that you don't think that Jake can go with you, were you to walk into the light. Why do you think that?"

"Oh my . . . sometimes you ask some tough questions, Roxanne! But let me take a stab at explaining that to you. Hmmm. Well, I see the light beckoning to me regularly. Nearly every one of your days. It's an incredibly pure white light. The first time I saw one of those newfangled LED lights, that's what it reminded me of. It's very prominent. There's just no way to miss it. There's no sound or anything, but it's pretty irresistible. The reason I think Jake cannot go with me into it is because when I see it, Jake doesn't. My light doesn't beckon to him."

"Ah . . . I see. That makes sense. If it's that obvious and irresistible, you'd be able to see him looking at it. Right?"

"Yes. One would think so. But he doesn't. Trust me, I've hoped he would every day. I've tried everything I could think of to get him to see it. No dice. Other human spirits, on the few occasions I've been with one when the light beckons to me, can see it. In fact, in every case they have gone to it. I remained."

"Huh. Weird. Can you give me an example? Do you mind?" I asked.

"Oh no. I don't mind. You see, it's not a sad thing to witness. It feels—good that they do. Right. Meant-to-be. For example, Mrs. Harper from two doors down. When she was having her fatal heart-attack, her daughter called for the ambulance. It came in fast, and made quite a commotion, so I walked over to see what was happening. As they brought her out the front door on the stretcher thing, I saw her spirit leave her body. They hurried to get her body into the ambulance, because they of course couldn't see that it had. Their machine didn't quit beeping until they were leaving the driveway. I guess it takes the body a few moments before it realizes it's dead.

"Anyway, poor Mrs. Harper's spirit just stood there watching the ambulance go screaming off, looking very confused. She noticed me and came right over. She hadn't walked under her own power in years, but she did then. She sure did. Didn't even seem to think about it. Just hurried right up to me, asking what had just happened. Before I had time to say a word, and just as her daughter came hurrying out of the house to her car, the light appeared just steps away from both of us. She looked at her daughter, looked back at me, and then walked right into it. It lingered for a few seconds beckoning to me, but when I didn't come, it dimmed and disappeared."

"Wow!" I'd heard story after story of people describing near-death experiences over the years, but I guess I kind of always doubted them. I mean, they just sounded sort of far-fetched. But here I sat, at Sam's snack bar talking to a ghost, and I had absolutely no doubt that he was telling me the truth! "So what about animals? What about Jake? You said he stayed here for you when he died. How does it work for them?"

"The same way, except for they have their own light. Theirs is a different color though. It's not LED white. Theirs starts out yellowish, like the first hint of sunrise on the horizon in the morning. Then it increases in intensity somewhat and becomes like every color in the rainbow. It's less frightening to them I suppose than our stark white light would be. That's what gives me the impression that it's a doorway to a different place than ours is. I'm sure you've heard tell about our beloved pets crossing over 'the rainbow bridge' to a place just this side of Heaven. I think that's where our pets go."

"Can you see Jake's light then?" I asked.

"No, not exactly. But I can tell when he sees it. He perks up like when he was alive, and I'd offer him a treat. He quits whatever he's doing, and stares at it longingly, just like he did his treats before I told him 'Okay' that he could have them."

I got up and fixed myself a cup of coffee. "Then how do you know all of what you just described?"

Elmer smiled his big, friendly smile. "Good question. Remember I told you that when I was alive, that I could See like you do?"

"Yes."

"Well, back then when his light would beckon to him, I learned that if I looked directly at Jake I could kind of see it out of the corner of my eye. Just barely, at the very edge of my peripheral vision. If I tried to look directly at it, it would disappear. I'm guessing it's a safety mechanism to keep the wrong kinds from entering the wrong light, but who knows for sure? Now I can't see it at all, but I still know when it's there."

"That makes sense," I agreed. "I'll have to pay attention to it and try to see it, if I see him acting that way."

Chapter 24

"Hey Jake? How about a walk to the park? Let's go see Toby!" I said, walking out the door, knowing he would follow. He did, staying right by my side the whole way there.

There weren't nearly as many dogs as usual and most of them were small, so Jake decided to lay at my feet in the sun and relax as he watched the gate and waited for his friend. I spread my things out on the bench beside me to discourage anyone else from sitting there. Phone, magazine, and my umbrella which I casually leaned against the seat. I had thought all of this out in advance, as usual. On the ground beside me I set out the two dishes I'd brought for Toby. One was for kibble and the other I poured a bottle of water into.

I had only made it about halfway through a random magazine of Sam's I'd brought to pass the time, when Jake let out a low growl. Looking up and around for Rand, Toby, or even another dog—whatever had Jake upset, I saw the very *last* person I expected to see headed directly for me. Steven!

Before he reached me, I was on my feet. So was Jake. He stationed himself in front of me, and his growling became louder the closer Steven got. Jake obviously remembered him and what he'd done the last time. "You stay away from me, Steven Bell!" I warned loudly, pointing a finger at him over the back of the huge black dog he couldn't see—or apparently hear.

That got the attention of several people who turned their heads and looked at us. They saw a woman standing alone by a bench who was obviously very upset, and a man who was stopped just short of her, pointing his finger at her and shouting. They hesitated to get involved, but continued to stare.

"I just found out what you did. How *dare* you treat my daughter like that? And getting physical with her? She came to the house to get *my* stuff, because I'm not allowed to, and you wouldn't even let her inside. You never did like her one bit, did you, Roxanne? You always gave her a hard time. You never gave her a chance."

I could barely hear Steven's words above the growls now. As Jake moved forward, he seemed to become more solid looking. He headbutted Steven in the lower chest, stopping him in his tracks. Steven looked down, clearly confused at what he'd walked into. Seeing nothing, he focused on me again.

"You know none of that is true, Steven. You let her mouth off to me every time she was around—you know what? It doesn't even matter now, Steven. When you hit me, that was the last straw. We're done, and you aren't supposed to be within three hundred feet of me! You either leave right now, or I'm calling the police and you're going back to jail!"

The people watching saw me reach down and pick up my phone from the bench. They saw Steven reach forward and snatch it from my hand. The one with the Ring of Protection on it. There was a giant spark—like static electricity, only *way* bigger. It knocked Steven away from me, but unfortunately made me fall down, as I wasn't expecting it. I'm sure to the witnesses it appeared that he'd pushed me down.

That made Steven even more furious, because it probably hurt like hell. As he got further away from the Ring of Protection, which had theoretically calmed his hatred of me somewhat in the moment, he took his frustrations out on my phone, making a big deal out of throwing it as hard as he could down on the concrete that surrounded the bench with a shout.

I'd hate to think what he may have done had I not been wearing these rings.

I'm sure everyone saw the phone explode into pieces. A few of the witnesses started moving towards me then. What they saw next must have confused them all. As Steven straightened up from demolishing my phone, he went flying backwards. Literally. He looked like a quarterback in a football game that a big lineman had just hit, without anyone slowing him down at all. He literally got *creamed,* except there was nobody visible to cream him. Then it looked as though something big grabbed him by the arm and was slinging his body against the ground by it. Except, again . . . there was nobody there. Everyone came to a screeching halt, at the vicious snarl that sounded after Steven's body hit the ground. Just like something had just released him. Because something had. Jake. But to them, there was absolutely nothing there.

The park fell silent. My would-be rescuers were seemingly frozen in shock as Steven jumped to his feet with that same wild look in his eyes I had seen before. As those eyes locked on me, I felt dread pool deep in my stomach. I stumbled back . . . just as a furious German Shepherd tackled him from behind, taking him down once again.

"Toby!" Rand yelled as he ran as fast as he could towards them. "Hold him Toby!"

Only Jake, Toby, and I heard him.

People were flat out running towards us from all directions now. They saw a man getting his arm mauled by a German Shepherd, who had him down on the ground.

"Let him go Toby! Release!" Rand commanded as he arrived on the scene.

Nobody heard him, they just saw the German Shepherd release the man's arm and back up towards me, where he stood snarling and growling at the man. Clearly, he was protecting me.

"Roxanne, are you all right?" Rand demanded, trying to catch his breath.

"Yes! That bastard isn't supposed to be within three-hundred feet of me! That's my ex-husband. The one who broke my jaw and put me in the hospital. Jake and Toby stopped him." Everyone heard me as they arrived at the scene, but I didn't care at that point.

"Toby stop! Stand down!" Rand commanded.

"Rocco you stop that!" screamed the not-doggie-mom-of-the-year Cruella Deville wannabe as she came running up, too. Reaching us, she slapped him on the snout with the leash she carried. Hard. Toby yelped, whimpering as he tried to hide behind me. That's when everyone got another unexpected and confusing show! As quickly as he had with Steven, Jake launched himself at Cruella for hitting his friend, with a terrible snarl that *everyone* heard. She flew backwards and landed on her butt with the wind knocked out of her before she could hit Toby again. "What kinda shit is going on here?" she whimpered when she could finally draw a decent breath again. "I didn't sign up for any of this craziness!" Hurriedly getting up, she ran for her van, leaving Toby behind without even looking back.

Our audience was stopped again, trying to figure out what had just happened. Steven struggled to his feet. "You'll pay for this, you bitch!" he screamed at me. There was a resounding SMACK, and his head snapped backwards. He dropped into an unconscious heap.

"You'd better learn some manners, mister!" Rand shouted down at him. But nobody saw or heard him, leaving some *very* freaked out people all around us.

Police sirens were quickly approaching the parking lot, and everyone stood where they were, waiting to see what happened next. Rand motioned to the leash the woman had dropped. "Toby's your dog and he was just protecting you. Everyone saw it. Don't let them take Toby away. Please!" he pleaded.

"I won't," I promised, as I snapped the leash onto Toby's collar.

A big man stood threateningly over Steven, apparently ready to prevent him from running off before the police arrived on the scene. Two younger women came over to me and convinced me to sit down on the bench, asking if I was all right and assuring me that they'd seen the whole ugly thing and would gladly tell the police that the man had attacked me. Their little dogs showed up yapping and running all around us. It turned into quite a circus.

Rand stood beside the big man watching Steven, who didn't know he was there, of course. Steven wouldn't be going anywhere, except back to jail. I don't know why, but I started crying. Jake came up from behind me, where nobody was, and put his huge head on my shoulder. My shoulder went icy fast, as his head passed right through, but I wasn't going to complain after what he'd done for me. Who knows, maybe it would even help stave off the bruising I knew would show up soon. "I'm okay big guy," I whispered to him. "Thank you!"

Two Grand Blanc police officers jogged up to us from where they'd had to leave their car. Everybody started talking at once, pointing at Steven and then at me. One went directly to Steven and hand-cuffed him. The other came to check on me.

"Are you hurt Miss?" he asked kindly.

Miss? I haven't been called that in over a decade.

"I think so. My ex-husband over there just scared me this time. I just got out of the hospital from the last time he attacked me. And—our divorce was just finalized. I'm sorry we made a scene. Please don't arrest me. My dog Toby was just keeping him off me. Please don't take him or anything." The tears rolling down my cheeks didn't even have to be faked, as I leaned down to hug Toby. I was that shaken—and angry.

"Your ex-husband won't be bothering you anymore today, Ma'am. We'll see to that."

"I have a personal protection order against him that's still in effect, signed by Judge Garland. It's in my bag right there," I said, pointing.

"May I see it please?" he asked. I handed it over. He looked at it quickly, turned to his partner who had Steven on his feet and said, "PPO violation. Assault with intent. Repeat offender." His partner nodded and turned Steven towards the patrol car, reading him his rights. Steven argued and complained as he was led away. I let out the breath I didn't even realize I was holding. I doubted very much I had to worry about *him* again anytime soon.

Rand came up beside me and put his hand on my shoulder. I jumped a little. I could feel it! *I have to remember to ask Rand about that.* Then it dawned on me—in order to hit Steven the way he did, Rand must have made himself corporeal. Solid.

***

It was a good hour later before the police finally left, taking Steven with them. I thanked everyone who had checked on me, gave statements to the police, and offered me rides home. I guess I only cried earlier because I was just *so* mad. I do that, I can't help it. But I was fine. In fact, I was better than fine. Suddenly, I felt like I had a team!

While I held Toby's leash, he and Jake horsed around in front of us. We all walked the black-topped path headed slowly towards Sam's house. "What happens now Rand? Cruella ran off and left Toby at the first inkling of paranormal contact. I'm surprised she didn't wet her pants. I kind of thought she would!"

He laughed. "Toby's better off without her. She just wanted bragging rights with her friends for having a 'rescue dog' because that's what they all do. She doesn't know the first thing about caring for an animal."

"Now it seems I have two dogs I owe big-time. And you . . . I can't thank you enough for defending me either." I reached out for his hand to give it a squeeze, but wound up sticking my hand right through it instead. "Hey, why could I feel your hand on my shoulder at the bench, but I can't touch you now?" I asked.

He laughed again. "Spirits consist of pure energy. That's why your hand just passed right through mine. I wasn't expecting you to try to touch me. Yours probably felt cold afterwards, right?"

"Yes."

"Depending upon how strong we are, we can solidify that energy momentarily. I may have overdone it with my fist earlier. Your ex-husband got smacked with something that may have felt more like a chunk of firewood than a fist, I'm afraid. Jake can do it too. Did you see how he flopped Steven around like a ragdoll? It takes a lot out of us to do that. He's playing with Toby right now, but deep down he's wishing for a nap."

"That's what Elmer told me. He said it took a couple of days for him to regain his strength. Does it make you tired too?" I asked.

"I barely feel it, but I'm a whole bunch younger than Jake, and I'm in really good shape. I mean I was."

"I hadn't noticed," I teased, winking, and then blushing like a sixteen-year-old girl instead of the forty-year-old divorcée I was. "But now you and Toby are homeless. Listen, I'm staying with my best friend, even though I have—had, a house right behind hers— ah, it's a long story. If I invite you inside, can you both be gentlemen while we figure this all out?"

"Absolutely!" he smiled.

I sure hope I know what I'm getting into!

"Elmer?" I called as we all entered the house, after making sure Sam's car wasn't in the garage. "We have company! Can you join us please?"

For once, he materialized where I was looking, right between myself and Rand. "Well hello friends! What a surprise this is. Welcome to m—to where we live." He smiled genuinely at them both. "Hi Toby. How's my buddy today?"

"He's probably still trying to get the taste of Steven's arm out of his mouth," I told him.

Startled, Elmer spun to face me. "Oh no, has something bad happened? Are you hurt again Roxanne?"

"No, no. I'm fine, but we have quite a story for you! You might want to sit down for this one."

Elmer relaxed and turned back to Rand, offering for him to sit down at the snack bar beside him. I moved around to the kitchen side, so I could face them both to talk. I held up my mangled phone to show Elmer, and then lay it on the counter somewhat disgustedly. Jake lay down in his spot in front of the slider and Toby got as close to him as he could without risking the frostbite sensation by touching him. They all appeared to be waiting for me to speak, so I did.

"We'd only just gotten to the park and settled in when Steven came charging right up to me . . ."

I recounted everything as accurately as I could for Elmer. I told them everything, including the verbal exchanges, my observations of the crowd, and all the details that Rand hadn't seen. The bit about the spark of power really caught both of their attention. I told them from my perspective what had happened when Cruella came running up and slapped Toby with the leash. "I was surprised when she got up. I thought she was down for the count! Jake had just about enough. She picked the wrong time and place to hit Toby that time! But—when she could get up, she ran off and didn't even look back. She abandoned Toby, like we'd hoped, but under different circumstances. Bottom line Elmer, Rand and Toby are here now. Sam is in for a surprise when she sees Toby. I'll tell her he saved me though, and she'll be more than fine with him staying. I'm sure of it. Everything worked out better than we could have hoped for. And Steven's back in jail!" I stopped at the end of my overly excited recounting, suddenly embarrassed. Maybe it was time to lay off the caffeine.

"Well, I, for one, am happy with how everything turned out," Elmer announced after a rather lengthy silent moment. He turned to Rand. "And how do you feel about all this, my boy? It seems to have affected you two even more than it did these two," he observed.

"To tell the truth, Elmer, I couldn't have imagined a better turn of events in my wildest dreams. That Roxanne has taken Toby under her wing alleviates all kinds of stress off of me. I'm good with it, sir."

"This needs to be said, so please don't take it in a negative way. This young woman here has been accepted into a very important position of responsibility in the paranormal world. I'll leave it up to her how much of that she wants to share, but more than that, she's respectfully fulfilled certain needs of my family that I was unable to. I owe much to her. My family owes much to her. In matters concerning Roxanne Bonacci, you will do well to remember that. Fair enough?"

"Yes, sir. Fair enough."

"Then, I guess it's time—" Elmer started, his voice choking with emotion. He stood up slowly and went over to where Jake lay in front of the sliding glass door. "Looks like everything has fallen right into place Jake. What do you think, old friend? Would it be all right with you if I went to check on Mama now that you have more friends to keep you company?" His voice cracking again. "Miss Roxanne promises to try to bring me back from time to time so we can visit. I miss your mama terribly Jake. Please forgive Daddy for what he's about to do."

Jake sat up and woofed softly. Elmer got down beside him on the floor and hugged him tightly, whispering something in his ear. Jake leaned away and woofed again softly, keeping his eyes locked with Elmer's, as tears flowed freely down Elmer's cheeks.

"Jake remembers his mama too, don't you boy?" Elmer said to—I guess all of us. Then he turned to me. "Well, I've been thinking about it nonstop since you mentioned it, Roxanne. Are you sure you don't mind?"

"Of course I don't. I owe my life to you two, and I would consider it quite an honor to spend my days in the company of such a handsome gentleman as Jake is. I have a question though. When he disappears on me, how will I know where he is, if I can't see him?" I'd already started sniffling.

"Oh, he'll still be right here. He won't run off anywhere. You'll show yourself when Miss Roxanne calls you, won't you boy?"

Jake woofed softly again, leaning his weight into Elmer and whining once. Elmer stood, bent, and kissed Jake gently on top of his head. He scruffed his ears once saying, "I love you Jake. I promise I'll never forget you. Come with me if you can, but if you can't, you be a good boy for Miss Roxanne. Look! There it is Jake! The light! Come on boy!"

Elmer glanced at me. "Look straight at me. Focus on me. Can you just see it out of the left corner of your eye?"

"I can!" I exclaimed, my own tears instantly flooding down my face.

With a little wave of his hand at me he repeated to Jake, "Come on boy," quietly. When it was evident Jake couldn't see what Elmer could, he slowly turned away. He looked back at the big dog, his faithful companion for so long, one more time before his attention was pulled back again. He called out softly, "Birdie? Here I come Birdie, my love!"

With a couple of large strides, Elmer disappeared. The room fell silent. Jake whined soulfully. I bawled, unable to stop. "Goodbye Elmer!" I called.

Jake cried and lay back down on the floor beside Toby. I went and sat next to him, wishing I could pet him or comfort him somehow. For the longest time, Jake stared at where he'd last seen Elmer. I wondered for the first time of many if I had done the right thing or not. How would I ever know?

Rand got up quietly and came over to me, putting his arm around my shoulders—hugging me. "Don't be sad. Be happy for him. You resolved all his issues and gave him what he wanted more than anything in the world. You even gave him the promise of trying to bring him back to see Jake from time-to-time."

"But, now my bringing Toby home with me has resolved your main 'issue', hasn't it? Does that mean you're going to leave me, too?" My eyes started to tear up. I couldn't help it.

Rand stepped in front of me, gently lifting my chin so my eyes met his. "I have a better reason than ever to stay here now," he said, kissing me gently, so I could feel it.

Forty may have been a wild ride, but age is just a number, right? And, who knows, maybe forty-one will be a truly fresh start. Pfft. Even I know better than that!

Ready for the next one?
SEEING WITCHY THINGS
amazon.com/dp/B089XKPFVL

Never miss a release date, contest, or giveaway!
Join my newsletter:
landing.mailerlite.com/webforms/landing/e0q4w3

Find me at:
amazon.com/author/leighraventhorne

facebook.com/Leigh.Raventhorne

(Guest Author in Paranormal Women's Fiction #PWF group on Facebook)

Thank you for reading SEEING DEAD THINGS. Please consider leaving a review on Amazon. That truly helps a new author sell books!

Manufactured by Amazon.ca
Bolton, ON